HOPE FOR FREEDOM

HOPE RANCH BOOK 4

ELIZABETH MADDREY

For anyone who needs the reminder that grace is for all of us. Even believers.

"I now pronounce you husband and wife. You may kiss the bride."

From her position as maid of honor, Indigo Hewitt smiled as her brand new brother-in-law dipped her sister Skye into a dramatic kiss. She joined in with the smattering of applause from the people sitting in the church sanctuary.

"Ladies and gentlemen, I present to you, for the first time, Mr. and Mrs. Morgan Young."

Skye and Morgan turned, beaming, and started down the aisle as the music picked up. Indigo took the arm Joaquin offered and fell into step beside him. She didn't see Royal and his girlfriend Sophie follow, but Indigo knew they were there.

Joaquin tucked his elbow closer in to his body, and Indigo fought the desire to shiver. He looked completely unaffected. Which meant she needed to be, too.

Easier said than done.

They exited into the foyer of the church, where Skye and Morgan had stopped near the door. Indigo released Joaquin's arm and hurried to her sister. "Congratulations."

Skye squealed and threw herself at Indigo. "This is the best day ever."

Indigo laughed and squeezed her younger sister. "I'm glad I could be here for it."

"That's part of what makes it the best. And Mom?"

Indigo frowned and gave her head a slight shake. "She wasn't feeling up to it."

"Right. Of course." Skye's shoulders drooped. "I guess that makes sense."

"It doesn't. I'm really sorry. I did try." Indigo patted her sister's arm.

"It's not your fault, Indigo." Morgan stepped closer and took Skye's hand. "It's not yours, either, Skye. And it's on her. Hopefully she'll come to the party at the ranch and at least be part of that."

"Sort of the opposite of what she did for Cyan." Skye nodded. "We'll hope she does. I'm not going to let her ruin my day. And we should form a line. The guests are starting to come."

Indigo stepped back, joining the receiving line next to Joaquin. She wasn't quite sure why she needed to be part of this —no one here knew her. They knew her sister. Or Morgan. But Skye had been adamant that all of the attendants were supposed to be in the receiving line. Since Mom was currently making everything as hard as it could possibly be, Indigo was determined to do her part to ease the strain.

"Do your cheeks hurt?" Joaquin leaned close, his breath tickled her ear.

Indigo chuckled. "So much. I think we're reaching the end, though."

"Good. I'm hungry."

"Food isn't for at least another hour. Pictures first."

Joaquin shot her a startled look before turning and offering a glittering smile to an old woman. "Mrs. Sandoval. I'm so glad you came."

"Joaquin, you're a charmer. When will it be you up there?" Mrs. Sandoval's eyes slid toward Indigo. "She's awful nice looking."

"She is, isn't she?" Joaquin winked at the old lady. "Have you met Indigo yet?"

"No, dear." Mrs. Sandoval shuffled to stand in front of Indigo. "It's lovely to meet you. You're another of Martin's children."

"Yes. Did you know my dad?"

"Oh honey, yes. I taught him Sunday school until he was in middle school." The woman frowned. "Not that it seemed to take. I heard he passed. I'm sorry for your loss."

"Thanks." Indigo's smile was tight and her heart hurt along with her cheeks. "It's been rough."

"Of course it has. For your mother, too, I imagine. She's not here?" Mrs. Sandoval peered down the receiving line.

"She wasn't feeling well." All Indigo had was the lame excuse her mom had made before closing and locking her bedroom door. There hadn't been time to push any more—not if Indigo didn't want to risk being late. But everyone was at least willing to try and accept it.

"That's too bad. Maybe I'll get to see her at the reception. I've always wondered what sort of woman would be able to keep Martin in line for so many years."

Indigo nodded and tried to mentally push the woman on. Mom hadn't kept Dad in line. That had come out last spring. And the whole family was still paying for it.

Morgan reached for Mrs. Sandoval's hand and pulled her into a hug. "I'm so glad you could come, Mrs. Sandoval."

As the woman moved down the line, Indigo let out a breath and turned away, her gaze meeting Joaquin's. "What?"

"Don't let her get to you. She's old and speaks her mind."

"It's fine."

He lifted an eyebrow.

"Really. It is. I'm worried about Mom. And actually I'm getting hungry, too."

Royal leaned over, joining the conversation. "Tell me. I'm starved. Skye said they'd have trays with food while we waited for the photos to finish."

"Aren't we in the photos?" Indigo wiggled her toes inside the high heeled shoes her sister had insisted she wear. They were starting to ache as well.

"Why would we be?" Royal's eyes were wide.

"Because we're the wedding party. Haven't you ever been in a wedding before?" Indigo glanced down at Skye. The last guest was on the way out the main doors, so Indigo stepped out of line and moved closer to her sister. "We're in the photos, right?"

"Yeah." Skye drew her eyebrows together. "Why wouldn't you be?"

Indigo chuckled and pointed at Royal and Joaquin. "They didn't know."

"Duh, Royal." Skye slipped her arm through Morgan's. "But we'll get the wedding party pictures done first. Then you can go eat while Morgan and I get a few extra couple pictures."

"That's something, I guess." Royal stuffed his hands in the pockets of his tux. "So let's get the show on the road."

Indigo bit her lip, trying to keep from laughing at his petulant expression. "I have a granola bar in my truck. Do I need to go get it?"

"Give him the keys. Girls are up first." Skye lifted the skirts of her wedding gown and headed toward the sanctuary, gesturing for everyone to follow.

Royal held out his hand. "You don't mind?"

"No, it's fine. It's open."

"You didn't lock your truck?" Joaquin frowned at her. "You're not in the middle of some hippie enclave anymore. You need to secure things."

"What?" She shrugged. "It's a small town and my truck is a rusted heap. If someone needs to break in to it, they're welcome to whatever they can find."

"Are they welcome to your truck?" Joaquin shook his head. "Start locking up."

"Check the center console. I should have a few choices. Get one for Grumpy here, too." She jabbed Joaquin in the chest before heading into the sanctuary and joining her sister and Sophie on the steps in the front of the room.

"Okay, ladies. That looks lovely. Dark blue dress, shift one step toward the bride and angle slightly."

Indigo followed the directions. Had her sister chosen different shades of blue on purpose to make it easier for the photographer? More than likely it was a little nod to Dad's naming conventions for the siblings—and it was kind of fun— but Indigo was grateful she hadn't ended up in the pale hue Sophie was sporting. If she had, it was inevitable that she would've found a way to stain it before the day was over.

"Eyes on me. Big smiles." The shutter clicked rapidly. The photographer lowered her camera and began rearranging everyone.

The guys filed in the back of the room, a broad-shouldered wall of black and white. Indigo's eyes drifted to Joaquin. He certainly filled out a tuxedo well.

"Okay. Groom?" The photographer glanced over her shoulder. "Can you join the ladies, please?"

Despite Skye's promise that pictures wouldn't take long, Indigo's feet had moved past aching to crying for mercy by the time she was finally walking toward the parking lot. She'd take her shoes off and drive barefoot back to the ranch. If she was lucky, she could stay barefoot for the bulk of the reception. It wasn't as if anyone was going to ask her to dance.

Would they even have dancing at a church wedding?

Indigo checked that her dress was out of the range of the truck's door before she closed it. She fished the key out of the cup holder—Joaquin would probably have something to say about that, too—and stuck it in the ignition.

A rap on the window made her jump.

She leaned over and cranked down the glass, her gaze on Joaquin's unsmiling face.

"You're lucky your brother is nice."

"I've always thought I was pretty lucky in my family, yes."

Joaquin snorted. "I was going to take your key. Or lock it in. You need to be smarter than that. This isn't Podunk Hippieland."

"So you've said." Indigo's spine stiffened. "I'll take it under advisement."

"Do that." He spun on his heel and stomped to his own truck. It was shinier. Newer.

If she had a truck like that, she might care enough to lock it up. With a mental shrug, Indigo turned the key, pumping the gas pedal when the engine hiccupped. It roared to life. Indigo rolled up her window before easing off the clutch and heading back to the ranch.

Joaquin might be easy on the eyes. And there was definitely some chemistry stirring. But apparently, he was a bossy jerk, too.

Now she had two goals for the reception. The first was to convince their mother to come. The second was to avoid Joaquin at all costs.

～

"ARE you sure I'm dressed okay?" Mom ran a hand over the simple black and white checkered dress she'd put on at Indigo's insistence.

"You look lovely." Indigo smiled and took her mom's arm, as much for moral support as to keep her from fleeing. "I know Skye's going to be glad you came."

"I should have gone to the ceremony."

"Don't worry about it. She understood." Or at least Indigo would try to corner Skye and make sure she told Mom she'd done so. Even if she didn't. Indigo wouldn't blame Skye for not understanding—what kind of mother couldn't at least try to get over herself long enough to celebrate her daughter? Maybe that was unfair. Her mother had had a rough year—first finding out about Jade, the child their father had with another woman. Then Dad's aneurysm. The summer had been filled with drama from Indigo, since her then-partner Wingfeather had literally gone into the desert and disappeared. Mom and Dad had both gone to Virginia for their oldest daughter Azure's wedding. But shortly after that, Dad had had a massive heart attack and died, leaving Mom with nothing.

Indigo had spent the last month helping her mom sift through the debris of her life now that Dad was gone. In the end, they'd sold the house in Arizona, and Mom had moved to Hope Ranch with Indigo.

Living with the parents your deceased partner had hated had to be stressful, too.

"Is that other woman here?" Mom scanned the crowd that was gathering in the main floor of the lodge.

"No, Mom. Skye didn't even invite Jade." She'd wanted to, but everyone had convinced her it was a bad plan. Especially right now, when they'd ended up splitting Dad's estate into six pieces instead of five. All of the kids but Jade had given the money right back to Mom. Jade, of course, had hung on to hers and made nasty noises about being owed more. Indigo sighed.

"I'm sorry. I should go." Mom tried to tug her arm away.

"Elise!" Betsy—or, maybe Indigo should call her Grandma like everyone else did—hurried across the space, a grin splitting her face. "I'm so glad you came. I've got the perfect spot for you over at our table. We can sit out of the way and watch the young people enjoy themselves."

"Oh. Well. I don't want to be a bother."

"Please." Betsy shook her head. "I promise you, I'll let you know if you ever manage that. You don't mind if I steal your mom, do you, Indigo?"

Actually, she did. Indigo studied her mom's face. Something in Mom's expression had Indigo pushing her lips into a smile. "No. Of course not."

"I just don't—"

Indigo leaned close and kissed her mom's cheek. "Go sit with Betsy and Wayne. I'm sure you'll have more fun with them."

Betsy patted Indigo's arm before looping her own arm through Elise's. "I snagged one of the trays of pigs in a blanket they were passing, so we don't even have to share."

Indigo chuckled. Mom was a sucker for those. How did Betsy know? With Mom settled—and Indigo was certain Betsy would see that Mom stayed for the bulk of the party—Indigo scanned the crowd for her siblings. Any of them would be fine.

Aha.

She skirted the edge of the room, barely noticing the exposed beam ceiling and big stone fireplaces that anchored each end. Tables were set up around a small dance floor in the center of the room. That answered that question. Her grandparents were not so religious that they weren't going to allow her sister to dance at her wedding.

"You look pretty good in a tux." Indigo slipped into the loose circle of people talking with her brother Cyan.

Cyan grinned. "You clean up pretty well yourself. I don't think I've seen you in a dress since you were twelve."

Had it been that long? Probably. Indigo shrugged. "It's not exactly conducive for animal care."

"Have you tried any of the food? If I can brag, I think I can safely say Maria outdid herself." Cyan leaned back and snagged a dumpling off a passing tray.

"She made all the food?" Cyan's wife was a wonder. "She's not too sick?"

"Not so far. A little morning queasiness, but she says it's not bad." Cyan beamed.

"Expectant fatherhood looks good on you." Her heart gave a little pang. She and Wingfeather had talked about kids. He hadn't said no—not firmly—but he'd never been excited. It had turned out to be a moot issue, anyway.

"You have to try these." Joaquin held out his loaded plate of appetizers and pointed to the dumplings perching near the edge.

"No. It's fine." They smelled like meat. Indigo smiled weakly.

"Maria made them vegan. For you." Cyan bumped her elbow with his. "Promise."

"Yeah? That wasn't necessary. But it's appreciated. I can go get my own."

"Don't be dumb. I got them for you. I mean, I tried one. It's food. They're good." Joaquin turned his plate so the little pile of dumplings was closer to Indigo. "Take one, then say thank you."

"Thank you." Indigo speared a dumpling and popped it in her mouth. Yum. Spicy cauliflower that mimicked the Asian pork that usually filled the doughy pillows burst with flavor on her tongue. And they were better than what was served at a lot of restaurants that touted vegan dishes. Unexpected.

She shifted her gaze over to Joaquin and drew her eyebrows together. How could a man go from being sweet to bossy and back to considerate so quickly? Coupling that with the sparks that zinged every time she was within six inches of him had Indigo taking a closer look.

Joaquin was a mystery she very much wanted to solve.

He turned and met her gaze. She grinned. "C'mon, Joaquin. Let's dance."

2

"Hey, man. I expected to see you at church." Tommy sauntered toward Joaquin's truck. "Want to walk up to the house together?"

Joaquin held up his fast-food bag. "I was there—sat in the back. I'm gonna stay in—watch some TV or something."

"You okay?" Tommy cocked his head to the side. "You look pale."

"Didn't sleep well."

"You getting sick?"

"Nah." In his heart, sure, but he wasn't going to explain that to anyone. "Just not in the mood. Can you give them my apologies?"

"Course. You know there'll be plenty if you change your mind?"

"Yeah. Thanks." Joaquin lifted a hand and hurried up the steps to his cabin before Tommy could press more. Tommy was his best friend here—honestly, his best friend ever—if Joaquin was going to be able to tell anyone without worrying about their response, it would be Tommy. And yet. Ugh. Not yet.

He turned the bolt—not everyone remembered to knock—
and hit the power button on the TV remote.

What was he supposed to do?

Joaquin unwrapped the first of three cheeseburgers and
frowned at it. His stomach twisted. Maybe it was hunger? That'd
be best case. He'd skipped breakfast. He couldn't skip lunch, too.
He took a bite and chewed, washing it down with a gulp from
the giant orange soda he'd ordered to go along with it.

Maria had probably made something amazing. It was getting
colder—there'd been a light dusting of snow on the ground
when he'd gotten up for church, though it was gone now. With
the way it seemed his luck was turning, she'd probably made
posole and he was missing it.

He took another bite and reached for some fries while
scrolling through the list of B movies he'd added to his queue.
Nothing leapt out at him. With a shrug, he arrowed up to the
show based on a comic that he'd started on a whim. He hadn't
taken the time to watch very many episodes—it was darker than
he'd expected, and the vigilante nature of the so-called hero
didn't sit well. He really wasn't in the mood.

He clicked the power and tossed the remote back on his
coffee table.

There was a reason he hadn't watched very many episodes.
His heart just wasn't in it. And at the end of the day, it didn't feel
like something Jesus would want him watching.

At least he could try and keep one area of his life on track
with God.

Joaquin leaned forward and braced his elbows on his knees
before covering his face with his hands.

He'd like to blame Indigo.

But it wasn't as if he hadn't been a willing participant in the
whole thing. And, if anything, seeing that he'd given his life to

Christ, and he knew for a fact she hadn't, it had been his responsibility to stop them.

To do better.

To be better.

He shoved to his feet and stalked into his bedroom. He stared at the messy bed, and the few bites of cheeseburger he'd managed to choke down threatened to come back up. He'd woken up alone, but her scent still lingered on the sheets.

He could fix that, at least.

Joaquin ripped the linens off the bed with more force than was necessary, sending the notepad and pens he kept on his nightstand skittering across the floor. He eyed the blankets and, with a shrug, scooped them into the armload of wash. He wasn't quite sure when they'd been laundered last, and right now seemed like a fantastic time to take care of that chore.

He hauled the load back through the living room and into the kitchen, where he dropped it on the floor in front of the pantry door that hid the stacked washer and dryer that Wayne had gone out of his way to have installed prior to Joaquin hiring on.

He closed his eyes. He owed his employer an explanation. Wayne was more than his employer. He was a friend. And a father figure. A spiritual mentor.

He'd let every single facet of that relationship down.

Biting back an oath, he opened the door and loaded the linens into the machine. The blankets would have to wait for a second load. It was fine. He had nothing but time.

When the wash was running, he went back to the bedroom and picked up the scattered items from his nightstand. He flipped open the notebook and scowled.

She'd left him a note.

Hey cowboy,

You look too cute sleeping to wake up. Had a fun time—let's do it again. Maybe moving to New Mexico was the right choice after all.

~Indigo

Joaquin ripped the page out of the spiral comb and crumpled it in his hand. He sank to the edge of the mattress and buried his face in his hands.

Oh, Jesus, what did I do? Can You possibly forgive me?

"MORNING, JOAQUIN." Wayne ambled up to the fence that enclosed the alpaca herd and propped a foot on the bottom rail. "Missed you at lunch yesterday."

Joaquin stopped raking poop, but just leaned on the rake where he was rather than closing the distance to talk more easily with his boss. "I'm sorry. I should've let you know."

Wayne waved that away. "Tommy said you didn't look like you were feeling well. You okay?"

No. He was absolutely not okay. He also didn't want to talk about it. He just shook his head.

"Okay. Well, you know I'm always here for you if you need me, right?"

"Yes, sir."

Wayne frowned and looked like he was going to say more, but Indigo called out.

"Hi, Wayne. Joaquin."

Was he imagining the little hint of secret knowledge in her tone? He cut his gaze over to Wayne. The man didn't look like he'd heard it. Or like he suspected anything.

"Hi there, Indigo." Wayne slung a companionable arm around her shoulders as she slipped up beside him. "Must be nice to have help with all these animals."

"It is. Frees me up some to focus on the fiber. I'm grateful, honestly. It's hard to juggle both. That was never the plan."

Wayne's eyebrows lifted. "Oh?"

Indigo let out a sardonic laugh. "Oh, no. Wingfeather was the one who was all hot and bothered to start the herds. I liked the idea well enough—it made dyeing and spinning and that whole process cheaper when the raw materials were right here. But the more success I got with the fiber end of things, the less he wanted to do with any of it."

One tiny thread of the knot constricting Joaquin's heart loosened. He moved closer to where the two of them stood. "I don't mind taking it all over."

She cocked her head to the side and studied him.

Joaquin fought the urge to look away. He could act natural. He *would*. Even if it killed him. He was going to have to talk to Wayne—explain, or, well, confess was the better word, everything—but it didn't have to be today. Or even tomorrow.

"You really don't mind?"

"Mind?" Wayne jumped in before Joaquin could. He gave a hearty laugh and squeezed his granddaughter close. "This one's been after me to add livestock to the ranch for a long time. You saved me from cows."

"Cows are a good investment." Joaquin shrugged.

Wayne nodded at Joaquin with a twinkle in his eye. "They are. They're a lot of hard work, too."

Joaquin shrugged.

"These guys aren't exactly easy." Indigo gestured to the pens of alpacas and sheep. "I'll take you up on it, Joaquin, if you're sure it's not going to keep you from your other duties around the ranch."

Joaquin shook his head. "I can handle it."

"I'll bet you can." The hint of sly knowledge in her eyes

made his gut twist. "You don't mind if I come visit them, do you?"

"They're still yours." Joaquin jerked a shoulder. "Do what you like. I need to get back to work."

"He's cranky today."

Joaquin barely caught Wayne's words as he headed back to finish cleaning the paddock.

He stiffened but kept his mind on the task. He wasn't going to get into it. And hopefully Indigo had the sense to keep her mouth shut about everything, too.

What would happen if she let it slip before Joaquin had a chance to come clean to Wayne?

He swallowed.

He needed to make sure he didn't find that out.

3

I ndigo stood at the fence and watched Joaquin as he worked. Wayne had headed back to the main house, but Joaquin had barely even acknowledged his departure.

Or the fact that she'd stayed.

She frowned.

Sitting around wringing her hands wasn't her style.

Indigo moved to the gate and lifted the latch, checking that it was secured behind her. She paused to pat the necks of Captain Janeway and Colonel Deering. Aeryn Soon and Starbuck were moving her way. She paused so she could give them some attention as well. Her gaze shifted over to the boys' paddock. They were milling around and seemed content. That was good.

Bidding the little group of alpacas goodbye, she closed the distance between herself and Joaquin. She shoved her hands in her pockets.

"Need something?" He didn't look up from his task.

"Are you sure you're okay taking over the animals like this? I wasn't trying to fob off my responsibilities. I realize you might have been on the spot with Wayne here."

"No. I don't mind. I like them. And he's right. I'd been in the final stages of convincing him to add some kind of livestock. Might even have been alpacas." He shrugged and started toward the little equipment shed.

Indigo fell into step beside him. "Are you mad at me?"

"No."

She waited. Surely there were more words that needed to go along with that short declaration. When he'd stowed his shovel and rearranged one of the shelves without speaking further, she sighed. "Kinda seems like you are."

"Look." He turned, arms crossed, face grim. "That shouldn't have happened. It's not going to happen again. We're not friends. We're certainly not more than friends. Just leave me alone, okay? You've done enough damage here."

Indigo took a step back. Her mouth opened and several words tried to form as her brain stuttered through the content of his tirade. "Damage?"

He nodded.

She poked his shoulder. "I don't recall you screaming for help, buster."

He held up his hands. "No. You're right."

"Darn straight I am. Damage. I'm not sure who you think you are, but it took two people to do that particular tango. I wasn't there on my own. If you regret it now, that's on you, but if you think I'm going to leave you alone when you're caring for the animals that make up my livelihood, you've got another think coming."

"Fine."

"Fine." She nodded once before spinning on her heel and stomping toward the gate. Damage. She'd like to show him damage. It was just sex. Good sex, at that, which made it a shame that he was too big of a toxic prude to have enjoyed it.

Or maybe it'd just been so long that she didn't know what "good" was like anymore. The rare times Wingfeather had been in town in the last eighteen months hadn't ended in him joining her at their place. No, he was happier crashing on a couch with his pals or visiting Irene.

She let out a growl. Irene.

That woman had been after Wingfeather since Indigo and he moved into the commune. Well, if he ever came home, Irene was welcome to him.

She glanced over her shoulder at Joaquin, shook her head, and checked that the gate had latched before heading back to the cabin she was sharing with Mom.

Hope Ranch. What a crock. The only hope here was that she wouldn't have to stay very long. Except it wasn't like she had a thousand other options.

"Hey! Indigo! Wait up!"

She stopped at the unfamiliar voice and saw her sister-in-law jogging toward her. What was the woman's name? Indigo fixed a smile on her face.

"Are you heading to the main house?"

"I wasn't planning on it."

"Oh." The woman's face fell. "Would you like to? I was hoping to get to know you a little now that you're here. I could fix some cocoa? I use real chocolate."

"Cocoa actually sounds really good." Better than listening to her mother grieve. Or if she wasn't in a grieving mood, complain. She needed to find a place to set up her shop, too. She huffed out a breath. "I forgot your name. I'm sorry."

"Maria." She grinned. "I should have realized. You got tossed in the deep end with the wedding, didn't you?"

Indigo shrugged as they walked past the cabins toward the stable. "I guess. I should have remembered more names though. You're family."

"I'll give you a pass this time. I think you'll like it here once you settle in some. It was overwhelming for me at first, too."

Maria pointed to the cabin just behind the main house. "When your grandparents set me up in there? Gave me a job? It was so much. So unexpected."

"That's Royal's place now, right?" Indigo studied the cabin and tried to picture her brother living there. The image wouldn't form. He, more than any of the sibs, was a diehard urbanite. "He likes it here?"

Maria laughed. "You sound as surprised as he was when he realized it. But yeah, he does. I imagine Sophie has a little bit to do with that, but he was making plans to stay even before the two of them got together."

"Are there more cabins?"

"Sure." Maria pulled open the back door to the main house and gestured for Indigo to go in. "Back where Cyan and I are set up there are a couple more. Something wrong with Morgan's old place?"

Indigo looked around the little mud room. She hadn't seen it on the tour Betsy gave her when she first arrived. "What? Oh. No. It's fine for living. The fiber work could use a little more room. I mean, I can take over the living room, but that doesn't seem fair to Mom. Or even if there was a spare room in here, if Betsy and Wayne wouldn't mind. And like I said, I can make it work. I'm not sure how Mom'll feel about it."

"Sure, that makes sense. Why don't I go bribe Betsy into hanging out with us and you can talk to her about it?"

"Oh, I don't want to b—" Indigo stopped talking as Maria hurried off. There were shoes on shelves against the wall. Was she supposed to take hers off? Maria had kept hers on. Everyone had worn them at lunch after church. She shrugged and moved through the kitchen to take a seat on one of the stools the lined the long counter.

Before she'd had time to do more than pull her cell out of

her pocket and open up her email, Betsy and Maria came back, laughing together.

"Hi, honey." Betsy wrapped an arm around Indigo's shoulders and squeezed. "I'm so glad Maria ran into you. And it's always a good time for cocoa. Have you been out without a jacket?"

"It's not that cold. I have a sweater."

"And it's lovely." Betsy rubbed the sleeve between two fingers. "Did you make this?"

Indigo nodded. "From the wool up. This was my first batch of the Finnsheep. I wasn't convinced that I was going to be able to branch out from alpacas, so only got four to begin."

"And now you're your own cottage industry." Betsy grinned and patted her hand before settling on the stool beside her. "Maria says you need more space."

Indigo hunched her shoulders. "I was trying to explain I could make it work."

"There's no need. We have room. The question is, how much do you need? And would you want a room here at the house or do you prefer to have private space where you won't be disturbed?"

"Just like that?"

Betsy angled her head. "Just like what?"

"You don't know me. Why would you do this? Why would you open your home and your heart without asking any questions?" It made no sense. Betsy might try to pull the family card, but really, that was just a matter of blood. Her father had made sure none of his kids knew anything about the people who'd raised him. Mom had gone along with it.

"Because what we have here is only ours because Jesus was generous to us. So we hold it with open hands and we share it where we can. Because that's what we're called to do. Aside from that, Wayne and I were always heartbroken by Martin's choices.

We missed out on so much when it comes to family. Having you and your brothers and sisters and now Elise, here? It's a gift beyond price. If we can do anything that makes it easier for you to decide to stay, we'll do it." Betsy reached for the mug Maria had placed in front of her and blew across the top.

Indigo took her own and stared into the chocolatey depths before raising it to her lips. She sipped. Her eyebrows lifted, and she glanced at Maria. "This is amazing."

"Thanks." Maria grinned and came around to claim a third stool at the counter. "Don't tell my son Calvin, though, would you? He's nine and can't have the sugar, and I haven't figured a way to make it diabetes friendly yet while preserving the taste. He considers it a catastrophe. I'll get there though. I've made it my mission for the fall."

"My lips are sealed." Indigo took another sip. It was strange to sit here with the grandmother she'd just met and her brother's wife of about a half-year. Strange, but pleasant.

"Back to the space. How much do you need? When we're finished here, I can show you some options."

"I'd like that. I kind of think I'd be better off not in the house. Then I wouldn't have to find yet another place to do the washing and dyeing. Carding, spinning, and packaging I can do anywhere, but the others take some space and have a mess associated with them that isn't suited for a living space."

"That makes sense." Betsy sipped her cocoa. "We'll wander out toward Cyan's place then and I'll show you the two cabins that are sitting empty. I'm sure one of them will work."

Indigo nodded. If they didn't, she'd just make do until she could figure something else out. The tool shed out in the paddock might be okay. It didn't have running water, which wasn't ideal, but maybe she could figure it out? She pulled her thoughts back in and concentrated on the conversation Maria and Betsy were having.

"They should be finishing the main structure next week." Maria shrugged. "Or so Sophie says."

"Hm. I wonder why no one mentioned it to me. Then again, Wayne probably knows."

"What are you building?" Indigo had seen the construction site, but hadn't given it a second thought. People on the commune were always tossing up a shed here or tearing down one building to make room for something different.

"Indoor riding ring." Betsy laughed. "Those aren't words I ever thought I'd associate with Hope Ranch. But Sophie is working on expanding her riding lessons and including some more therapeutic options, and it's better for consistency if they can go year-round. Around here, that means they'll do better with protection from the elements. It's not going to be a lavish space, but it'll be heated and dry."

"That's really nice of you." Indigo drained the last of her cocoa and shifted to face her grandmother. "We never really discussed rent and such before I came. Would I have that conversation with you or with Wayne?"

"Neither of us. We're glad you're here."

Indigo shook her head. "No. I'm using up land with the animals. And Joaquin's time, since he was telling Wayne this morning that he was happy to take over their care. You pay him and now he's doing work for me—either I need to pay you, or I should work something out with him directly."

"Indigo—"

She held up a hand. "Wait. Please. You've given me and Mom a place to stay. Plus now maybe another of your buildings for me to run my business out of. I make decent money with my fiber— over and above what it costs to care for and invest in the herds. Please let me pay my way here."

Betsy sighed. "You're your father's daughter, aren't you?"

Indigo shrugged. "Is that bad?"

"No, honey. No, it's not. I'll talk to Wayne, and we'll get a proposal together. I'll warn you now, I don't think we're going to accept rent for your living in one of our cabins. We're happy to have family here on the ranch. We have the space, and we're thrilled that you can use it."

Indigo nodded slowly. She could sort of see that. "Okay. As long as you let me pay for the business and the rest."

Betsy nodded. "Like I said, we'll get something put together. It'll be easier once we know where you're going to set up. Why don't we take that walk now and give the free cabins a look?"

"I'd like that." Indigo slipped off her stool and picked up her mug. She carried it around and rinsed it out before setting it in the sink. "Thanks for the cocoa, Maria. It was delicious."

"I'm glad." Maria hesitated before adding, "Could I come along? I don't need to get lunch started yet and I wouldn't mind a little walk to get the blood flowing before I dive into the rest of my work."

"Of course." Betsy patted Maria's arm and stood. "Let me grab my jacket from the front hall, and then we'll go see where our new fiber business is going to be located."

4

J oaquin double-checked the harness on the two horses that were hooked up to the sleigh. There was just enough snow on the ground that it should pull their Friday evening guests without any hiccups. Maybe it was a little less snow than they usually had on the first weekend of December, but it was enough.

"All set?" Wayne rubbed Cinnamon's nose and tilted his head at Joaquin.

"Yes, sir."

Wayne's eyebrows lifted. "You know, I'm starting to think you're avoiding me. You've been scarce at lunch all week. What's going on, son?"

Joaquin's heart sank. He had been avoiding the main house. It seemed like the easiest way to stay out of Indigo's line of sight. And that was absolutely necessary for everyone's sake. He'd talked to the pastor on Wednesday. He shook his head.

"If you're trying to tell me nothing's bothering you, I'm going to be sad about it, but I'm still going to call you a liar."

Joaquin closed his eyes. "No. I can't talk about it right now."

"Right now or yet? Or ever?"

He would love to choose ever, but it wasn't realistic. Sooner or later, he was going to have to come clean. Sooner was better. The pastor had been very clear about that. He swallowed. "I don't know."

Wayne frowned, his eyes full of sorrowful concern. "Okay. I won't ask again, but you know I'm here. You're part of our family, as far as either Betsy or I are concerned. You know that, right?"

Joaquin met Wayne's gaze and nodded. He did know that. It made his transgression a hundred times worse.

"All right then. You remember Tommy's setting up at the westmost path this year. We've marked a good number of trees for folks to choose from for the cut-your-own tree. They'll have a color-coded bracelet that they need to match to a tree tag—that way they only cut the height range they paid for. You're still good with helping out the folks who can't manage the saws?"

Joaquin chuckled. There were always families that thought it would be fun to cut their own Christmas tree who got started and then discovered it was more work than they'd bargained on. "Yeah. Between Tommy and me we should be fine."

"Betsy and I will either be down at the big house checking people in or over by the bonfire helping with s'mores."

"I thought that was Calvin's job."

Wayne grinned. "It is. But how am I supposed to sneak marshmallows if I don't go over to try and help?"

That was a fair point. He'd need to be sure to get over there himself. Maria would have hot chocolate—not the amazing cocoa she made for the family and ranch staff, but it was still better than the powdered packets he kept in his kitchen. The temperature was dropping as the sun lowered and painted the mountains red. Hopefully, the families wanting to cut a tree would get here soon. There wasn't much worse than trying to saw in the dark. They had another two hours, tops, before it'd be too dark for that portion of the evening.

"This is something else." Indigo, arms crossed over her chest, sauntered his direction. "Sophie said you do fall festivals now, too?"

Joaquin tamped down on his temper. Maybe she was trying to be nice. Friendly even. Didn't she understand he wasn't interested? Oh, sure, physically she was basically the incarnation of his dream woman, but she wasn't a believer and he'd already proven he couldn't be trusted around her. But he could be polite. He'd have to be, since Wayne was watching without even bothering to pretend he wasn't. "This year was the first year for that."

"And the sleigh rides?"

He shrugged. "Been doing them since before I came."

"Which was when?"

"Maybe ten years ago?" Had it been that long? He'd been twenty-two when he showed up hoping to get hired on. He'd wandered to Taos on a vacation after finishing college. He was supposed to go home and get a job at his father's company afterward, but he'd never wanted the suit-and-tie nine-to-five life, even if it held more security. "Yeah, about that."

"Interesting. It looked like there was a decent sized crowd heading this way."

Joaquin glanced toward the main house where Wayne and Betsy would be collecting the tiny fee they charged for an evening of winter fun. "Good. Even though Skye's managed to get the camp operating more in the fall—and I think she was saying there were bookings already in January and February— it's a tight margin around here."

"Was that a dig?"

"What? No." He frowned at her. Why—and how—would it be a dig? "It was a statement. One meant to convey to you the fact that, despite how ridiculous you clearly think it is, our Friday and Saturday sleighs and s'mores during December are an important part of keeping the ranch running."

She held his gaze for several heartbeats before she nodded. "Sorry."

"Fine." He broke eye contact. Nothing good was going to come from gazing into her eyes. They were too captivating by half, as history had already proven. As much as he might like to be part of the love and marriage tsunami that was sweeping through Hope Ranch, it wasn't going to be with Indigo. She wasn't his type. She wasn't a believer. And he was pretty sure they weren't even going to be able to manage being friends. "Did you need something else?"

She sighed. "I was actually going to try and take the first sleigh ride. I thought it might be fun and a good way to see more of the ranch. Is that a problem?"

Yes. A huge one. "We might be full."

"Betsy said the first one was usually the emptiest."

Darn it. Betsy was right. That was most often the case. His frown deepened and he jerked his head toward the sleigh. "Might as well get in and take a seat."

"Gosh, thanks." Sarcasm dripped from her tongue as she fluttered her eyelashes at him before rolling her eyes and hoisting herself into the sleigh.

Joaquin clenched his jaw.

"Here come guests. Maybe you should try to look less like someone who's going to drive them out into the woods and murder them." Indigo was leaning over the edge of the sleigh, watching him.

He glowered at her. That woman was a walking example of why physical attraction didn't make a relationship worth diving into. He ran his hand down the neck of the closest horse before stepping around them and closer to the path that the little clump of people was walking up. "Sleigh rides?"

A little girl jumped up and down, dragging on her mother's hand.

Joaquin's heart softened. He squatted down so he was at her eye level and smiled. "You excited to go for a ride?"

She nodded vigorously. "And we're gonna chop a tree down. I didn't know Christmas trees could be real."

He grinned and stood. "They're the best kind. You need to help your mom keep it watered though, okay?"

"Okay!" The little girl scrambled into the back seat of the sleigh and her mother hopped up after.

A couple more people stopped to say hello and verify they were in the right place before climbing in.

Joaquin looked down the path. It was devoid of groups for now. He might as well get this run started. If nothing else, it'd get it over with sooner.

He hopped in, stepping over Indigo to get to his spot. How had she ended up next to him? Last he checked, she'd been in the middle. He glanced over his shoulder and saw a four-person family had occupied that spot. Well. "It was good of you to move and let the family sit together."

She laughed. "You don't have to sound so surprised."

He shrugged. He was surprised, might as well let it leak through into his voice. "Git up!"

The horses stepped out, bells on their harnesses jingling.

"Are we supposed to sing?" Indigo nudged his side with her elbow.

"Nope." Sometimes people did, but it wasn't something he started off. "I'm not a cruise director. I just drive the horses."

"Do you point out the features of the ranch at least?" Indigo nodded toward the sheep and alpaca pens. "People might enjoy knowing what you do up here. And the fact that they can now get hand-dyed, hand spun wool if they're into knitting."

He shook his head. As far as he was concerned, one of the best parts of being on sleigh duty was that the folks in the back were content to talk amongst themselves and leave him alone. It was a good time to think. Or just let his mind wander. And there was plenty of beauty to look at. "Not everything needs narration."

"Not all silence is golden."

He glanced over at her sour retort and bit back a smile. Maybe they could've been friends if they hadn't messed it all up right out of the gate. Now they'd never know. No use worrying about it. She was too dangerous for him to even try to meet in the middle. It'd be like trying to keep a rattlesnake as a pet.

"Excuse me. Are those alpacas?"

Joaquin saw Indigo twist in her seat and smile. "They are."

"Have you given any thought to working with 4H at all?" The man scooted forward a little on his seat. "We have a handful of kids who'd like to form an alpaca club, but it's a bit more than their parents are ready to bite off."

"What's involved?" Indigo reached for her long braid and flipped it over her shoulder. "I might be willing."

"Basically, it's a chance for kids to find out what it takes to care for the animal as well as participate in shows. Let me give you my card. If you think you might be interested, you give me a call and we'll talk. I guess maybe I should've gone to Wayne, but I didn't realize you had animals."

Indigo smiled and took the man's card. "They're new. They're mine."

"You a grandkid?"

Joaquin chuckled under his breath. Now, after all that, the man was interested in who she was? Talk about putting the cart before the horse.

"I am. I moved here with my mother and my herds about a week ago. Well, the herds actually moved out here toward the end of September when my dad died."

"Heard about that. Sorry for your loss."

Indigo's smile looked tight. "Thanks. Anyway, Joaquin's been doing a good job taking care of them, which frees me up to focus on the fiber business they supply."

Joaquin pulled back on the reins and the horses slowed to a stop near where Tommy was set up with a table holding crosscut saws for families to use. "This is the tree-cutting stop. If you've paid for a Christmas tree, Tommy here will help you know where to look and how to identify the tree you want."

Everyone but Indigo climbed down from the sleigh.

Joaquin slanted her a look. "You're not getting out?"

"I don't need a tree." She gave him a big, toothy smile. "Besides, the company's so pleasant, why would I give that up?"

He shook his head. So much for a quiet ride and the chance of avoiding conversation. There'd be another group waiting to get on the sleigh when he got back. By the time he loaded them up and made the return trip to Tommy's set-up, there'd be one or two people ready to make the round trip with their trees, and if Indigo had gotten out, he would have been able to avoid being alone with her.

He could ask Tommy to swap. Boy, was that tempting. But then Tommy would ask questions—and demand answers—and that was the exact opposite of what Joaquin intended to do to push that night with Indigo out of his mind forever.

"Suit yourself." He fought a sigh and raised his voice so it would reach Tommy and the families clustered around him. "I'll be back in a bit. Take your time. We do the circuit until everyone's finished and at the main part of the ranch. Git up!"

The horses started up. It was easier to just complete the scenic circuit than try to turn the sleigh around. Even if the first part of the trip was a tad shorter.

"So. You really hate talking to me that much, huh?"

"I don't hate talking to you." A horrible thought flitted into his brain. "Could you be pregnant?"

"Wow, that's a change of subject."

"Yeah, well, you're not answering me, either." Joaquin stared straight ahead and focused on keeping the horses where they were supposed to be going.

"I can't get pregnant." Her voice was tight and her body stiff.

The wave of relief that rolled through him almost made him drop the reins. "That's good. Okay. It's all going to be all right."

Indigo let out a huff of air and shifted, still stiff as a board, so that she was facing away from him.

What was that about? He shook his head and focused on the group of folks waiting for the sleigh not too far in the distance. His heart was lighter and Joaquin breathed a prayer of thanksgiving. He'd messed up—no question—but it seemed as if God was going to forgive him after all.

5

I ndigo sat at her spinning wheel, her foot moving on the pedal at a steady pace while she pulled the roving out and twisted it onto the bobbin. Pull and twist. Pull and twist. It was soothing. She needed to get a Bluetooth speaker so she could have music that wasn't coming through the tinny little one on her phone.

She'd been at Hope Ranch almost two weeks. It wasn't what she'd expected. Of course, she hadn't really known what to expect. Dad had painted such a different picture of her grandparents than appeared to be reality. Sure, they brought Jesus into every conversation, and the whole "won't you come to church with us, dear" thing was going to get old, but they weren't mean about it. And they'd let her say no twice now.

Honestly, they were so casual about the whole thing, she was tempted to give it a try this weekend just to see what was what.

"Knock, knock. Can I come in?" Elise poked her head in the door of the cabin Indigo had taken over for her fiber.

"Sure, Mom. Push on the door when you close it though, would you? It sticks a little." She needed to see if Wayne had a file she could borrow. It'd be easy to fix. If she forgot to check that it closed, the draft got chilly fast. "What brings you out this way?"

Mom shrugged and shook snowflakes off her coat before hanging it on a hook beside the knitted poncho Indigo had worn on the walk over. "Needed a change of scene."

Indigo glanced up and raised an eyebrow.

Her mother's cheeks pinked. "Fine. I'm hiding from your grandmother."

Indigo laughed. "I imagine this is going to be the second place she looks for you, if she drops by our place and you're not there."

"Maybe. But it was all I could think of." Her mom glanced around the room. "You don't have anything to sit on?"

"Sure, there's a chair in the dining room, through there." Indigo stopped spinning so she could point to the archway that led to what would be a dining area. She was using it to hang yarn to dry after she'd dyed it. Betsy had said there was no problem putting screws in the ceiling, so Indigo had suspended her drying racks. It felt like they took up less room that way. To her, at least. But she needed to stand on a chair to reach the top rungs.

Mom came back with the hardbacked chair. "This looks comfy."

Indigo smiled at the dry sarcasm. "Sorry. You can fold up my poncho and your jacket as a cushion. It's on my list to make this place a little more welcoming, but I'm behind on my spinning orders, and I wanted to get caught up on that, first."

"It's okay. I don't mean to pick." Mom looked around the room and shook her head. "How'd you even learn to do all this?"

"YouTube, mostly." Indigo shrugged before moving the yarn to a new hook on her bobbin to spread the yarn over the whole area. She gave the wheel a little push and started her feet on the treadle again. "Then a lot of practice. Trying things and failing, making tweaks and trying again. The same way you learn to do anything, I guess."

"It's impressive. The yarn you have drying, is that all yours?"

"If it's on white drying racks, yes. If it's on the ones I painted red it's for a client."

Mom nodded. "You were always smart."

Indigo smiled. That was high praise from Mom. "Thanks. I like to think my parents taught me not to be afraid to try new things."

Mom chuckled. "I'm not sure we taught you, we just didn't give you any other options."

"Same thing, when you boil it down." Indigo paused to reach for a new section of roving. She caught her mother watching her and lifted an eyebrow. "Want to give it a try?"

"Oh, no. I'm sure that's too important. You said it's for a customer." Her mom waved her hands.

Underneath her mom's words, though, Indigo heard the hint of interest. "The wheel isn't really the place to start anyway. Let me get you a drop spindle and some roving that I don't think is going to dye up very well."

"I don't want to ruin anything."

"You can't ruin this. If it's bumpy, then it'll just be rustic when you knit it up." It would be bumpy. The first try at spinning was always bumpy. Usually the second and third tries, too. Indigo rummaged through a box until she found one of her drop spindles and some scrap yarn.

"Knit? I don't knit."

"We'll work on that next." Indigo brought the spindle and the roving over to where her mom sat and showed her how to tie the scrap yarn to the hook and wind it around the bobbin. "Now, you twist it up like so, feed some of the roving on, and slowly let it out as the spindle turns. See?"

Her mom watched, a little crease of concentration between her eyebrows. "I see it. I'm not sure I can do it."

"Well. You won't know until you try, right?"

Mom laughed. "Got me there. All right. You watch for a minute, okay, and make sure I'm not messing it up?"

Indigo crouched in front of her mom and watched the agonizingly slow process. She nodded. "You've got it. Now wind the spindle up again and do some more."

Mom squinted and bit her lip as she worked through the motions again. "I'm doing it."

"Don't sound so surprised. I never had any doubt."

She laughed. "I did."

Indigo grinned and returned to the spinning wheel. This yarn was spinning up nicely. They wanted a double-ply when all was said and done, so once she'd spun the roving onto two bobbins, she'd spin in the opposite direction to twist the two strands together. It wasn't hard. Just time consuming. She could still make the return time she'd given her client, but it was going to be closer than she liked. "If you get good at that, I'm going to hire you on."

"Would you? Do you think there's a way I can help here?"

"Sure. There's always something to do. What about your lotions and candles though?"

"Oh, I don't know. I just did that so I had something to do when you father would go off on a ramble. Now?" Mom shrugged. "I don't have many orders coming in—I never have. It's not like I can make rent doing that."

"Rent? What do you—"

"Hello?" Betsy knocked on the door and grinned as she stepped in. She gave the door a solid push when she'd closed it, then rubbed her hands together. "Oh, how nice. I wondered where you'd gone off to, Elise. I didn't realize you could spin, too."

"I can't. I'm just learning." Mom set the spindle in her lap with a strained smile.

"Oh, don't let me interrupt. This is quite an operation you've got, Indigo. You described it all, but seeing it is different. Can I look around?"

"Why don't I give you the tour?" Indigo stopped her wheel, set the roving aside, and stood. "Mom, you want to come?"

"Oh. Well." Mom looked down at the spindle she still clutched in her hands before setting it aside. "Sure."

Indigo gestured to the living room. "Eventually, I'd like to build some shelves for the walls in here and make a display area in addition to having my spinning wheels set up. I need to talk to you and Wayne about whether or not you'd be okay with some retail hours."

"I don't see why not." Betsy grinned. "I imagine you could get quite a few people who'd be happy to come up here to shop for the sort of yarn you're making."

That was the hope, certainly. Online sales were never an issue—she listed the yarn on her own website as well as on a popular craft website. Synching the inventories was a bit of a pain—she made a mental note to email her web designer and ask if there wasn't a way to automate that—but so far the extra work was worth it. "Okay. Thanks. Um, through here is the dining room. I've turned it into the drying room."

Indigo led the two women through the archway and tried to see it as they would. "I hung the racks from the ceiling—you did say that was fine."

"It is. Did you make these yourself?" Betsy reached out to brush a finger across one of the floor-to-ceiling racks.

"Yeah. Um, Wingfeather helped a little. They're just PVC pipe."

"It's ingenious." Mom glanced at Betsy, who nodded at her.

"Your mother's absolutely correct. It is."

"Well. I don't know about that, but it gets the yarn dry. I was telling Mom, the white ones are all my personal stock. The red are the yarns I dye for clients." She tucked her hands in her pockets and searched her mind for more to say, then shrugged. "Come on into the kitchen."

Metal steam pans, strainers, and stock pots were drying on towels on the countertops.

Indigo moved into the kitchen and started stacking them together. "Sorry. I did some dyeing on Monday and left these to dry. I didn't clean up—I wasn't expecting—"

"Indigo."

Indigo stopped at Betsy's words. "Yes?"

"Do I look like I'm upset that you're using the space like you told me you were going to?"

"Well, no. But I could be tidier."

Betsy laughed, loud and full. "Couldn't we all. If this is how you need to leave things to make it convenient for your business, then do that. I'm not the clean-up police, I just like seeing what you do and how. Maybe some time when you're dyeing you'll let me know and I can watch."

"Oh. Um. Sure." Indigo set the steam trays back down. "I'll have to get another respirator. There can be fumes, and you don't want to mess around with that."

"Well then, let me know." Betsy patted Indigo's shoulder. "It doesn't look like you have a lot of other special equipment?"

"Not really. You don't need it. I have a wish list, of course, of things I'd like when I can justify the expense. But for now, these are great." Indigo gestured to the doorway. "I've basically got boxes in one of the bedrooms. The other is empty. I think I can use the bathrooms for washing fleeces, but I might also be better off with livestock water troughs outside. I'll have to see what I need when I get to that point. The lanolin can muck up the pipes if you're not careful, and I'd hate to do that to you."

Mom smiled. "I imagine it's more that you don't want to do it to yourself."

"That, too." Indigo shrugged. "I need to get a table to set up my drum carder. Sooner than later on that. And Mom pointed out that I could use a little bit of furniture for people who come to visit."

"You should talk to Royal. Or Skye when she and Morgan get back from their honeymoon. I'm guessing either of them could help you find something over at the camp lodge or online that would work." Betsy went back out into the living room area. "This is something else, Indigo. I'm so proud of you."

"That's what I said." Mom picked up her spindle and sat back down.

Betsy eyed Mom's movements. "Do you think if I went and got myself a chair, you could teach me to do that, too? Do you have the supplies?"

Indigo laughed. "Yeah. Sure. I'd be happy to."

"I'll be right back."

When Betsy had gone out the front door, Indigo watched her mother spin. Her yarn wasn't super bumpy—there was room for improvement, but it wasn't bad at all. "You're getting good at that. What did you mean about rent?"

Mom sighed. "I don't like mooching off your grandparents."

Indigo nodded. "I feel the same. I think, between you, me, and this fiber business, we can work something out. You're okay staying here, though?"

"You know what? I am. I didn't think I would be. But it's nice here. Sometimes I realize your father was a bigger idiot than I thought."

Indigo laughed. "Oh, Mom."

"Okay." Betsy dragged a chair through the doorway. She must have gotten it from someplace close. Had she stopped over at Cyan's to borrow one? "I'm dying to give that a try. Show me what to do."

Indigo rummaged through the box for another drop spindle and set her grandmother up. For the first time in a whole lot of years, her heart was light. Maybe, just maybe, her life was finally coming together.

6

"You got an enemy I don't know about?" Tommy jabbed Joaquin in the side with his elbow before laughing.

Joaquin frowned. "What do you mean?"

"You were taking an awful lot of notes during the sermon. I just figured if you needed to write that much about loving your enemies, it must mean you've got one. Care to share?"

"Just because you can't be bothered to take notes, doesn't mean the rest of us shouldn't. In fact, I'd venture to say I'll remember more of the sermon in a week than you will by the end of the afternoon."

Tommy snorted and reached for the knob of the main-house back door. "You think so? I guess we'll see."

Joaquin shrugged and stepped into the mudroom. He paused to wipe his boots on the rug before continuing through to the kitchen. He couldn't stop his smile when he saw Maria and Cyan wrapped up in each other in front of the stove.

Tommy ran into him. "What's the—oh, hey guys. Smells good, Maria. We eating in the dining room again?"

Maria and Cyan broke apart.

Maria's cheeks flushed scarlet. "Yes. I think that's going to be the case going forward. Betsy says it's better for big family meals."

Joaquin nodded. Family. The Hewitts had always treated him like family. He cringed when he thought about how badly he'd betrayed them. Forgiven. He was forgiven. He'd confessed his sin to Jesus, and that was all it took.

Why couldn't he let it go and move on?

He dragged his thoughts back to the present and saw Tommy leaving the kitchen. He turned to Maria. "Can I help at all?"

"You okay, Joaquin?"

"Yeah. Of course." He forced a smile and prayed it was convincing. "But I've got two empty hands just waiting to be filled."

"If you want to grab that stack of plates and go set the table, it'd be a help. And Calvin will owe you fifteen minutes of his time this week to make up for you taking over his chore. You think you could find something for him to do with the sheep? He keeps nagging me about going over to see them, but I'm just not sure about them."

Joaquin's eyebrows lifted. "You're not sure about the sheep?"

Maria shook her head.

Cyan laughed. "She thinks they're plotting something. Says their eyes are shifty."

Maria swatted at Cyan with the kitchen towel she'd had slung over her shoulder. "They *are*. You mark my words."

"I'd be happy to have Calvin help me with the sheep any time. Just send him down and we'll find something to do." Joaquin hefted the pile of plates and flatware.

"My sister treating you right?"

Joaquin nearly dropped his armload when Cyan spoke. He cleared his throat. "Uh. Sure. I guess."

"Those animals are like her babies. If she gets obnoxious, let me know. I'll dunk her head in a bucket."

"I don't think I'm going to get in the middle of whatever sibling issue this is. I've got a table to set."

Cyan's laugh followed Joaquin through the doorway.

Tommy was sitting next to Indigo at the empty table. He'd leaned over close and had his flirting face on.

Joaquin's teeth ground together. "Maria could use more help, Tom."

"Oh, please. She never wants help."

Indigo shifted, angling her body away from Tommy. Why didn't the man see that she wasn't interested? Tommy was probably just playing around, anyway. He didn't even date—his ex would make his life a living misery, or more of one, if she caught wind that he had someone serious in his life.

Joaquin set the pile of plates on the table and moved the flatware off the top.

Indigo jumped up. "I'll help you."

Before he could say no, she'd moved over and scooped up the flatware, her arms brushing against his. "Why don't you go that way with the forks and I'll head around the other direction with the plates?"

She shot him a quizzical look but shrugged and laid out a place setting.

Joaquin dropped a plate between the fork and knife and moved away from her. He shouldn't be attracted to her anymore. She was off limits for so many reasons, the foremost being her spiritual state. Being his bosses' granddaughter was a close second.

"I have a question about that sermon this morning." Indigo glanced up from where she was aligning a spoon beside a knife.

A plate clattered to the table. "You went to church?"

She nodded. "I didn't want to go with Betsy and Wayne.

They took Mom, though. It just feels like a lot of pressure to go with them."

"I could have given you a ride, if I'd known you were heading down." Tommy leaned back a little, but Indigo still had to get close to set the silverware out at his spot. "Where is everyone else?"

"Cyan said Betsy wanted to introduce Mom to a few people. They should be here soon." Indigo scooted around Tommy's seat and bumped Joaquin's side. "Anyway, do people really do that? Love their enemies?"

"Supposed to, yeah." Joaquin looked up and met Indigo's piercing gaze. He swallowed and dragged his eyes away. "Not always easy."

"I was wondering—" Indigo broke off when a door some-where slammed and Betsy called out that they were home.

Running footsteps pounded down the hall and Joaquin heard Calvin talking animatedly with his parents in the kitchen, though he couldn't make out the words.

Joaquin set the last plate down and slid from the room. He nodded to Betsy, Wayne, and Indigo's mom as he went back to the kitchen to see if there was more to do. Anything had to be better than talking about a sermon on loving enemies with Indigo.

He didn't want to love her.

He didn't want them to be enemies, either.

He was a mess.

The meal was loud. Sundays at the Hewitts' had always been loud, but the more actual Hewitts who showed up, the louder it seemed to get.

Joaquin kept his head down and tried to keep from shoveling the food into his mouth too fast. Maria was an amazing cook—gulping it down wouldn't do it justice. And it wasn't as if he could excuse himself without having to explain.

He didn't have an explanation.

His gaze kept flickering over to Indigo. She didn't look as if she was enjoying herself, either. Should he try to engage her in conversation? Tommy, at least, had given up trying to flirt. That eased some of the tension in Joaquin's stomach.

When everyone's plates were clean and conversations had started to wind down, Wayne scooted back his chair and started to stand. "That was delicious as always, Maria. Thank you. Do you want help with the dishes?"

"No. I've got Calvin on KP with me." She reached over and ruffled his hair.

"Aw, Mom." The boy frowned.

Maria laughed. "Up. Help me clear."

"I wondered, Joaquin, if you and Indigo could join me in my office for a few minutes?"

"Oh, Wayne, no business on Sunday." Betsy reached for his hand.

"It'll just be a minute." He patted Betsy's hand then stepped away and nodded toward the door.

Lunch suddenly wasn't sitting too well. Betsy had said business—did she mean it? Hopefully, yes. Otherwise . . . well, it didn't stand thinking about. If Wayne had found out about them would he deal with it in his office like this? Joaquin didn't know.

He really didn't want to find out.

He stood and followed Wayne from the room, avoiding Indigo's gaze. Did she know what this was about?

"Take a seat. I won't take up much of your afternoon, promise." Wayne leaned back and his desk chair let out a piercing squeak. "Keep forgetting to spray some WD-40 on that. Maybe I'll get to it this afternoon."

Indigo peeked in.

"Come on in. Pull up a chair." Wayne pointed to Betsy's office chair. When Indigo was seated, she scooted the chair away from

Joaquin's. Wayne's lips twitched but he didn't comment on the action. "Indigo, Betsy mentioned the conversation you had with her about rent. Seems she had a somewhat similar conversation with your mom recently, too. I hate that you feel obligated to pay us."

"It's not an obligation." Indigo butted in. She shook her head. "But I'm using your resources and it's only right that you benefit from that. Or at least that you don't get taken advantage of."

Joaquin's eyebrows lifted. He hadn't expected this, at all. None of the Hewitt grandchildren had shown up and expected to be taken care of. It was unreasonable for him to have assumed Indigo would be the first who did. But he needed that list of reasons she wasn't the woman for him. And yet the cons kept getting scratched off.

"I guess that's all in how you look at it, but I admire anyone who wants to do for themselves. Betsy mentioned a primary concern was Joaquin's time—the cabin and the space for the animals is easy enough to work up a rent that will be reasonable for both of us. So I thought maybe you'd have some ideas about the best way for you to be reimbursed for your time, Joaquin."

Reimbursed for his time? He shook his head. "I don't need money. You pay me well, Wayne. Caring for the stock isn't taking time away from the work you need me to do—maybe I've rearranged my schedule some, but I'm still pulling my weight."

"Never thought otherwise." Wayne smiled. "But my granddaughter feels you ought to have some compensation for your work."

Joaquin frowned at Indigo. "What if I say no?"

Indigo's frown deepened to a scowl. "Why would you?"

"Because I like having animals on the ranch. I like being involved in their care. Wayne, you know I was lobbying for this —I never expected extra income from it. Just a little extra work to fill my time. You and I both know you don't need me *and* Tommy. One of us would be more than adequate to handle the work we do."

Wayne chuckled. "I wasn't sure if you knew that."

"I do. Tommy does. We're both grateful that you're willing to keep us on." Joaquin laced his fingers together to keep his hands from shaking. Was his job in jeopardy? Or Tommy's? "What if, when you're figuring out the rent for the land, you just add a little extra in for animal care and call it a day. I don't need it passed to me. Fact is, I know you and Betsy run Hope Ranch with tight margins—use the extra to loosen them up a little. Or don't. But let it be between you and Indigo."

Wayne gave him a long, measuring look before turning to Indigo. "Does that work for you?"

"If he's sure." She turned to Joaquin. "Are you sure?"

Joaquin gave a single, sharp nod.

Her shoulders fell. "Then I guess it's fine. It feels wrong, but if everyone's happy, who am I to complain?"

"Is that all?" Joaquin stood. He didn't need to be here while Wayne and Indigo figured out the rest.

"Sure. Thanks." Wayne reached for Joaquin's arm as he passed. "Are you okay?"

Joaquin glanced over his shoulder at Indigo then back at Wayne. "Yeah, of course."

Maybe if he kept saying it out loud, he'd get to the point where it was true.

7

Indigo wove the tail of yarn into the sweater and held the finished garment out in front of her. She'd left this yarn natural—it had an interesting variegation of browns from the alpaca that she hadn't wanted to risk messing up. Or having to bleach. All things considered, it was going to make a lovely gift for her grandfather, and she'd finished it just in time. Christmas was only five days away.

The thought was ever-so-slightly nauseating.

She didn't do big family Christmases. Half the time she'd been with Wingfeather, she hadn't even realized it *was* Christmas until one of her siblings called to say hello. Even then, she didn't always answer the phone, so she'd find out whenever she got around to checking her voicemail.

She stood from the old sofa Betsy had had hauled over from the camp lodge. She'd gone to the cabin she shared with Mom one night and had come back in the morning to find the couch against the wall with a note from her grandmother. It was ugly, but comfortable, and at some point, Indigo would knit a throw or two to go over it, and that would solve the ugly problem.

For now, she needed to get this sweater blocked. She went to the back room where she'd set up a table. The cardigan in deep purple wool, spun and dyed from her Finnsheep, was already laid out. She rested her hand on it and smiled. Completely dry. It was soft and gorgeous, if she said so herself.

Indigo folded it and set it aside. She carried the sweater for her grandfather into the attached bathroom and filled the tub with cool water. She submerged the sweater and squeezed to make sure it got wet then left it to soak for a moment while she went back into the bedroom to fetch a towel. She spread it out on the floor before removing the sweater from the tub, laying it on the towel, and carefully rolling them up. She stepped on the roll and slowly walked down the length then back, letting the towel absorb the moisture out of the garment.

"Indigo?"

"In the back bathroom, Mom."

Footsteps echoed down the hall, then her mom poked her head in and furrowed her brow. "What are you doing?"

"Getting ready to block the sweater I made Wayne."

"By stepping on it?"

Indigo laughed and picked up the towel. "It gets the water out. Come see."

"Why'd you make Wayne a sweater?"

"Christmas." She paused in the middle of unrolling the towel and looked at her mom's face. "We can say it's from both of us."

Tears shone in her mother's eyes and she looked away. "I hate this. I hate being dependent on the Hewitts and on my children. And I hate your father for putting me in this position."

"Oh, Mom." Indigo turned and wrapped her mother in a hug. She knew a little of what her mom was feeling. Hadn't Wingfeather done the same to her when he abandoned her in the commune? She hadn't been able to care for the herds and even pretend to stay on top of her spinning. She'd managed, sort of, but she'd relied on a lot of help from the others, too. "I'm sorry."

Mom shook her head and stepped back, wiping her eyes. "Don't be. You've done more for me than you needed to. You wouldn't mind if I shared your gifts? I could pay you for the yarn or something?"

"No, Mom, you don't have to do that." Indigo crossed the room to a tissue box and pulled out a couple that she took back and offered. "You've always done so much for everyone, I'm happy to share. Let's get this on the blocking board and I'll show you the cardigan I made Betsy."

"Is that the purple?"

Indigo nodded.

"That's a lovely color. I'm sure she'll be thrilled."

"I hope so. Wayne set such a low fee for the land and this cabin, it still doesn't feel right. I want to repay them somehow, but he's stubborn. I see where Dad got that part of his personality."

Mom laughed. "Betsy is, too, so he got a double helping."

Indigo smoothed Wayne's sweater out on the blocking board, tugging here and there to adjust the stitches and make them even. She stuck a few pins in to keep it in place and stepped back. "Now it just has to dry, and it'll be great."

"How are you doing with your spinning?"

"I'm almost caught up. I have one more bag of fleece to process. I thought I might go ahead and open up orders. It'd be good to start collecting again. I have some of my own fleece from the spring still to deal with, but they aren't going to make money immediately, so I'd kind of like to alternate and keep the income steady until I figure out the retail end of the in-person yarn shop."

Mom settled on the sofa. "Have you thought of offering lessons?"

"What kind?" She didn't particularly want to teach people to card and spin and dye. That would cut into her business. It didn't seem smart to offer classes on the things you hoped to sell.

"Knitting? Crochet? Some of what I've seen in your boxes looks woven—do you do that, as well?"

Hm. That was an idea. She could teach all those things—except, of course, it was time consuming. The time she spent doing that was time she wasn't processing wool or making things herself. "I hadn't thought of that, no. And I did have a loom. It seemed like too much hassle to move, so I sold it in Arizona. I could always buy another if it was something I wanted to get back to."

"I used to weave, a little."

Indigo studied her mom. "Do you miss it?"

"I don't know. I always used a pattern, so I don't think it's something I have a talent for. It's not as if I made up designs and brought them to life."

"When was this? I know we never had a loom on the school bus."

Mom laughed. "Wouldn't that have been something? No, do you remember the classes I'd take? That was one of them—I think it was when we spent that long stretch of time on the California coast."

When Dad was busy with his second family that he never told anyone about. Indigo bit her lip. "If you want to give it another go, let me know. We'll find us a secondhand loom and set it up."

"I'll think about it." Mom smiled. "You showed me the sweaters for your grandparents. What else have you made for Christmas presents?"

She'd stored them all in the back room. Indigo turned to go get them and bring them out, and the room wavered. "Ooh."

"Are you okay?"

"Yeah. Just a little lightheaded. Must've turned too fast. Or not had enough breakfast." Indigo reached out and braced one arm on the wall to steady herself. The thought of food made her stomach turn unpleasantly. She swallowed back the queasiness.

"You should sit."

"No, Mom, I'm okay." Indigo drew a deep breath in through her nose and held it for a five count before letting it out. It helped some. Hopefully she wasn't getting sick. "Let me go get those gifts."

THE SUNDAY BEFORE CHRISTMAS. Indigo scooted along the wall of the big main room they called the worship center. Were there worship sides, too, that this was the center? She didn't really understand the terminology. She liked to sit about halfway to the front of the room, but over on an end of the row by the wall. It seemed more anonymous than the back row, where everyone was sneakily looking during the welcome and greeting time.

And wasn't that the world's most awkward two minutes of each service? She'd become the champion of tight smiles and firm handshakes without revealing anything about who she was and why she was there. No one pushed. It was all "Hi, so good to see you!" She could practically see the exclamation points at the end of their sentences.

Mostly, she just wanted to avoid running into Joaquin or Tommy. Well, Tommy was out of the picture for a few weeks at least. Apparently, he spent Christmas in Colorado hoping to see his daughter. His ex sounded like a real piece of work. But Joaquin was still a possibility.

"Hi."

She glanced up and fought a sigh. Speak of the devil. "Hi."

Joaquin gestured to the empty seat beside her. "Can I sit with you?"

"Why?"

He blinked. "Because it's the last Sunday before Christmas and it's the time of peace on Earth and goodwill to men?"

Her lips twitched and she moved her knees to the side to make a bit more room as he stepped past her to the seat. She tried not to stare at his rear end—but it was right there and so very ogleable.

"You shouldn't ogle butts in church. Pretty sure that's a thing." Joaquin's whisper was light and his eyes danced with laughter.

"I'll keep that in mind. Is that in the Bible? Maybe you could text me the reference?"

"You're reading the Bible?"

Indigo tapped her phone's screen so it brightened and showed the app she'd downloaded and had open.

Joaquin's gaze was searching. Whether or not he saw what he was looking for, Indigo couldn't quite decide, but he nodded. "Do you want a paper version?"

She shrugged. She'd considered buying one—it was easy enough to add to one of her online orders. The church had also mentioned that they'd be happy to give her one—well, not her specifically, just the pastor offered it to anyone at the end of every service. "The app works for now. This way I don't lose it."

"Fair enough. Can I ask what you've been reading?"

The praise band—that was what everyone called them, so Indigo went along with it, but it made her squirm. Was praise part of their name? Like the Steve Miller Band? Or was it what they were doing?—came onto the raised platform at the front of the room. And she'd learned the hard way that it wasn't to be called a stage. Even though it was one. The main guy who sang, because Indigo wasn't going down the confusing mental rabbit hole of *his* title, invited everyone to stand and worship the Lord.

She stood and focused on the screens on either side of the big bathtub at the front.

Joaquin's elbow dug into her side. "If you haven't hit it up yet, try Mark. And then John."

"I started at the beginning. Isn't that how you read a book?" Everyone around them started singing. Leave it to her to read the Bible wrong.

"You can. It's just maybe less confusing if you don't." Joaquin smiled. "There's no wrong way to do it."

That helped. She nodded and pressed a hand to her stomach. She really wished the nausea would stop. It was like she had low-grade food poisoning. Except, of course, it came and went. Altitude sickness, maybe? But no, she didn't have trouble breathing. She was just tired and queasy.

Tired. And queasy.

Oh, no.

Bile worked its way up Indigo's throat. She swallowed, her hand flying to cover her mouth. *Nononononono . . . this can't be possible.*

Indigo grabbed her purse and lurched out of the row. She half stumbled, half ran to the foyer, her eyes desperately searching for the restrooms. There, at last. She slammed her hands into the door and raced into a stall, barely making it before the meager contents of her breakfast came back up to see daylight a second time.

When she finished, she sat back against the stall door and lowered her head to her knees. If she'd ever wanted proof that God didn't exist, this was it.

Tapping at the door, then a squeak. "Indigo? Are you all right?"

Joaquin. Of course he'd followed her. Because he was a nice

guy. Even though he'd distanced himself from her at the ranch and had a snarky tongue, at his core he was good.

And she'd ruined him.

"Yeah. Fine. Go back to church, Joaquin."

"I'm still at church." She could hear the smile in his voice and her lips twitched in response. "I, uh, happened to catch the tail end of what you're doing in there. You're not all right. You got the flu or something?"

Or something. Definitely or something. She tried for casual. She didn't know for sure. Except, of course, that it was glaringly obvious. "Probably just breakfast didn't agree with me. I've never been the world's best cook. Part of why I went vegan."

He chuckled. "Do you want me to run you home?"

"No!" She took a deep breath and tried to visualize blowing out the panic that clutched at her chest. "No. Thanks. I've got my truck. I'll be okay."

"You're sure?"

Why wouldn't he go away? She pushed to her feet, flushed the toilet, and stepped out of the stall with a wan smile. "I'm sure. I'll just wash my hands and head home. I probably just need a nap."

He frowned, but nodded. "All right. Would you text me so I know you got there okay?"

She closed her eyes as the warm water rinsed bubbles off her hands. Definitely a nice guy who deserved so much better than the chaos she always brought with her. "I don't have your number."

"That's easy to fix." He held out his hand.

It was easier to go along with it. She could argue—but they'd just end up here longer, and she really needed to get to the drugstore. She slipped her phone out of her pocket and handed it to him. After a moment, he handed it back. "I sent myself a text. So you just have to add another under it, okay?"

She nodded and forced a smile, hoping it didn't look as sick as she felt. "Thanks. I'll see you. Could you let Betsy know I won't be at lunch?"

He studied her again. Did he know? Or guess? Indigo fought the urge to squirm. Finally, he gave another, slower nod. "All right. Be safe."

"Yeah. Thanks." Safe. If she'd paid attention to safety in the first place, neither of them would be in this situation now.

God? Are You there? I don't really think You can be . . . but if You are? I'd really love to be wrong right now. A little help?

8

J oaquin checked the water trough in the alpaca shelter. There was plenty in there. The animals themselves didn't seem to mind the cold. Some were wandering around in the paddock and nosing at the snow. Others stood in clumps under the shelter. Overall, they seemed happy.

Which was more than he could say for Indigo.

He blew out a breath and stared toward the cabins. Was she okay? She'd texted to let him know she'd made it home—but it seemed like it took longer than it should. He'd completely missed the sermon because he'd been looking at his phone and waiting for her text.

Should he go see her?

At lunch, Maria had offered to send a plate home with Elise. So Indigo should have gotten some lunch. Rest was probably all she needed.

He should leave her be.

It wasn't as if they were more than passing acquaintances. But still. He reached out to scratch the head of the brown alpaca who came over to investigate. He didn't usually spend a lot of time just standing around in the paddock, so he understood her curiosity. Joaquin looked at her fuzzy brown face. Was this Captain Janeway? He thought so. Indigo could tell them all apart at a glance. He didn't know them well enough for that yet.

With a final rub on the alpaca's head, he made his way to the gate. He'd go back to his own cabin and fire up the Xbox. Maybe Tommy would be online and the two of them could fight some battles together. In fact, he pulled his phone from his pocket and tapped out a quick text. Maybe Royal would want to play. He and Sophie tended to spend Sunday afternoons together, most often at her parents' house, but sometimes they'd join in. Would Morgan and Skye want to play? Did people still basically on their honeymoon, for all they were back in town, want to play video games with friends on lazy Sundays?

Joaquin checked that the gate latched and strolled back toward his cabin. He paused in front of what used to be Morgan's place but now housed Indigo and her mom. No. He had a plan. He'd stick to it.

A few more steps took him home. Inside, he hung his coat on one of the pegs by the door, tucked his boots under the little bench, and wandered into the kitchen. He grabbed a bag of chips and made his way to the living room to fire up his game console.

After a brief internal debate, Joaquin grabbed his phone and texted Indigo.

HEY. JUST CHECKING ON YOU. FEELING ANY BETTER?

Three dots bounced at the bottom of the screen. Then they stopped. No message though. They started bouncing again and her message appeared.

NOT REALLY. DO YOU HAVE A MINUTE TO TALK?

SURE.

CAN I COME THERE?

Joaquin's eyebrows lifted and he glanced around the living room. It didn't look terrible. But was it wise for her to come over?

Last time had been a bad idea. He shook his head. No. He wouldn't make the mistake again. And he had Tommy and Royal waiting to play Xbox. That was a good safety net.

Sure.

Okay. Be right there.

Joaquin shot Tommy and Royal another text telling them he might be a few minutes. He'd barely finished sending it when there was a rapid knock on the door.

He went to open it and frowned. "You look awful."

"Thanks." She hugged her arms to herself. "Can I come in?"

"Yeah, sure. Sorry." He stepped back and let her in, then closed the door behind her. She was pale still, and her eyes had taken on a hollow, haunted look. "Can I get you some water? Or tea?"

"You have tea?"

Joaquin rubbed the back of his neck. Did he? "I used to. Want me to look?"

"That would be nice." Indigo pulled a chair out from the small table in the kitchen and sat. She cradled her head in her hands.

Joaquin rummaged through the box of random drink mixes and unearthed two tea bags. Did tea go bad? He had no idea how old they were. What would going bad even mean when it came to tea? "Peppermint okay?"

"That actually sounds really good." She looked up with a weak smile. "Thanks."

"No problem." Joaquin filled mugs with water, plopped the tea bags in them, and stuck them in the microwave.

Indigo winced.

"What?"

"It's nothing. Tea snob stuff."

"If you're a tea snob, you're going to be unhappy with my tea bags anyway. I don't actually know how old they are. Would you rather just have water? Or a soda?"

"It's fine. Just, so you know, microwaving the water won't get it hot enough. Or it'll be uneven and too hot in some places. But it's no big deal."

If he stirred the water when it was done, would that help? And really, who knew there was supposed to be a specific temperature for tea? Tea snobs, apparently. The microwave beeped and he grabbed the mugs and carried them to the table. "Do you want sugar?"

Indigo grabbed the string of the tea bag and slowly dragged it back and forth. "No. This is fine. Or should be."

He sat and mimicked her movement with the tea bag. He usually just dunked it up and down, but he could play along. Maybe doing it this way would somehow make it taste better? Tea had never really been his thing. He couldn't quite place why he had any. "So."

"Right." She cleared her throat then lifted the tea and took a swig. "Oh. Hot."

He smiled and blew across the top of his before sipping. He wrinkled his nose. It still tasted like hot minty water. Why did people drink this?

Indigo took a deep breath and blew it out before lifting her gaze to meet his. "I'm pregnant."

Joaquin's eyelid started to tick. He squeezed his eyes closed and fought the feeling of falling down a deep hole. "I'm not sure I heard you right."

She looked down. "You did."

"I thought you said—"

"Yeah, well, that's what I always thought. Wingfeather and I tried for years. Nothing."

Joaquin took a long drink of his tea, wincing at the taste. He shoved his chair away from the table and went to the fridge for a

Coke. Twisting off the bottle cap, then let the sweet bubbly liquid soothe his desert-dry throat. They'd been so caught up in the moment, he hadn't thought. If he'd thought, he would have been able to step back. Step away. Stop before things went all the way.

"I'm sorry."

He glanced at the table. She was sitting there, head bowed, fingers twisted together. What were they supposed to do? He ran a hand through his hair before dropping into his seat. "What now?"

"I don't know." She looked up, then away.

"We'll get married." The words tasted like dust, but they felt right. He added a firm nod for form. "We can go into town tomorrow, and—"

"No." She jumped up and paced away from the table, still wringing her hands. "I'm not even sure I believe in marriage. This isn't Regency England, where you have to save my reputation. I can take care of this baby. Or . . ."

"There's no 'or,' Indigo. Please don't do that." He didn't have the power to stop her, if it was what she chose, but how would he live with himself if she did? "I want to be involved. I'll be a father to this baby—even if you don't want to get married, you can't push me out of his life."

"Or hers."

"Or hers." One corner of Joaquin's mouth lifted. "I'd be fine either way."

"I'll think about it."

She could think all she wanted; he wasn't backing away from this. One massive mistake wasn't going to snowball into more. "It's not open for discussion."

"Sure it is. This is my baby." She came to the table and sat, reaching for her tea.

"*Our* baby. I have rights."

Her lips thinned as she pressed them together. "Why are you acting like this? You've been pushing me away since my sister's wedding."

"Because what we did was wrong, and I didn't want to repeat it. This changes things."

She shook her head. "No. It doesn't. This is my problem."

"Don't try to shut me out, Indigo. I don't want to have to get lawyers involved, but I will."

"You're *threatening* me?" She stood up so fast that her chair clattered to the floor. "Seriously?"

"It's not a threat. I'm this child's father. I will be supporting him or her. I will be part of their life." He clenched his teeth together. That was non-negotiable. Period. And he was going to be on top of this from the beginning, not like Tommy. "If you don't want to get married, we're going to co-parent. Fifty-fifty."

Her mouth dropped open. "You don't get to decide that."

"I'm pretty sure I have a say in it. I *am* the father, right? There's not someone else it could be?"

Indigo let out a short scream.

"Look. Spend time with me, okay? We know we're attracted —why don't we find out if there's more to it than that and go from there?"

"I thought you weren't going to be involved with me because of the whole Jesus thing." She smirked and crossed her arms.

There was that. But maybe, just maybe, if she spent time with him, she'd start to see Jesus, too. Missionary dating wasn't the best plan, but Joaquin needed to be part of his baby's life. And he'd like to do it as a husband—to let his child grow up in a family with both parents around all the time. He did some quick mental calculations. "You're due in what, August?"

She blinked. "I don't know. I just took the test today. It's not like I've been to the doctor yet."

"Nine months, right? So August. Ish. Forty dates."

"What do you mean?"

"Go on forty dates with me. One a week until the baby's born."

"Why?"

"To see how we're going to make this work." Joaquin closed the distance between them and did what he'd been longing to do since he first woke up and realized the mistake he'd made. He took her hand and held it to his heart. "I want to be a father to my baby. Please, let's see if we can make it work?"

"One a week?"

He nodded. "Working with the animals together doesn't count."

She frowned. "Fine. No kissing."

"What?"

Indigo shrugged. "You made a demand. That's mine. No kissing. I'll go on your dates—I guess I sort of see that it makes sense for us to get to know each other if you're going to be a hard a—um, stubborn—about this. But I don't understand why you can't be like most guys and be fine with not having responsibility dumped in your lap."

Joaquin offered a sardonic smile. "I've never claimed to be like most guys."

"Yeah, well. Lucky me." She tugged her hand away from him and scowled. "With Christmas this week, I doubt I'll be able to get to the doctor. But when I do get an appointment, do you want to come?"

"I do."

"Maybe you could choose different words, okay?"

"I'd love to come along. Let me know the details, and I'll drive you."

"I can drive."

He held up his hands. "Okay. You can give me a ride."

Sighing, she nodded. "I didn't plan this. I want you to know that."

"I believe you." He paused a moment. He wouldn't have chosen this. Ever. It was basically the complete reverse of how things were supposed to go. And yet. "It's going to be okay, Indigo."

She headed toward the front door and turned with her hand on the knob. "I hope you're right."

So did he.

9

"Are you feeling better?" Mom looked up from her seat on the sofa in their cabin. She was working her drop spindle and the natural roving was spinning into a much more even yarn than at first.

"That looks good, Mom. Let me see." Indigo crossed the room and took the spindle. She ran a finger along the yarn—still a few bumps, but well within the margin allowable for home-spun. "We can sell this, if you want."

"Really?" Mom took the spindle back and looked at it then back up at Indigo. A slow smile formed. "I . . . wow."

Indigo grinned in response. It was good to see Mom excited about something. Happy. Really happy for the first time since August. "We'll two-ply it and look again, but this is nice, Mom. Good job."

"Thanks." Mom took a minute to twist the spindle and start adding more roving. "You didn't answer my first question though. Everyone asked after you at lunch. They're all going to pray for you to feel better."

Indigo sighed. "I'm fine. I got some news that shook me."

Mom simply lifted her eyebrows.

She might as well say it—it wasn't as if she'd be able to hide it forever. "I'm pregnant."

"Oh. Well." Mom blinked several times before folding the spindle and roving into her lap and lacing her fingers together. "Not Wingfeather's. Obviously not. Someone here?"

"Joaquin. After Skye's wedding—it was just a thing. A mistake, if you talk to him."

Mom scowled. "He's already trying to wiggle out of it. Of course he is. All men are jerks."

"No. Mom, no. Actually, he's pretty insistent that he's going to be involved with the baby whether or not I want him to." She flopped against the back of the couch. "What am I supposed to do?"

"What do you mean? You give birth and raise your baby. With Joaquin. You must like him at least a little, if you slept with him, right?"

Yes, she liked him. When he wasn't being obnoxious. And apparently the obnoxiousness was his defense mechanism because he was attracted to her and didn't want to be. Long lasting relationships had started with less. They'd forged some kind of footing, maybe it could even be called a friendship, when they'd chatted about alpacas and sheep. Now, she guessed they'd see if they could actually make something out of it. "Yeah. I guess I do."

"That's good then."

"He asked me to marry him." Sort of. It was more like he'd told her they would get married. But she understood the gist.

Mom laughed, stopping only when she studied Indigo's face. "You're serious?"

Indigo nodded.

"What did you say?"

"I said no. Of course, I said no. It's ridiculous."

"It's not. Not necessarily."

"Mom. No."

"You could always abort. That's never been something I'd do personally, but it's an option."

Indigo's hands settled over her abdomen. She'd entertained the thought very briefly. But she'd always wanted a family. Wingfeather never had—but he'd been willing to see what happened. Even though it turned out the answer was "nothing." She'd assumed it was her.

Apparently not.

"No. I don't want to do that. I can raise a child. I think I'll be a good mom." Indigo smiled at her mom. "I had a good role model."

Mom patted Indigo's hand. "I'll support you no matter what. And help how I can. Honestly, I might be better at that than anything I could do to assist your yarn business. Babies, at least, I know."

"You're doing great with the yarn, Mom. And I know you'll be a big help with the baby." She frowned and bit her lip. "Do you think Betsy and Wayne will still let me stay?"

"Yes."

"Just yes? No qualifications?" Could it be that easy?

"I think so, yes. The longer I know them, the more I realize how completely ridiculous your father was about them. They're good people. And this Jesus thing—I think they mean it. They're not like some of the Christians you run into who use their religion as a reason to look down on you or explain all the places you don't measure up." Mom shrugged. "Their church is different than I expected, too."

Indigo nodded. Joaquin's church wasn't anything like she expected, either. "Do you think Dad was wrong about that, too?"

Mom sighed. "Yeah. I guess I do. The past three weeks I've sat in church next to your grandparents and listened for the condemnation I expected to hear. Instead I heard about love. I don't have a problem with the idea of sin—you raise kids, you're going to run into the fact that human nature isn't inherently good. But even that idea of sin isn't something they're pulling out to make you feel guilty or extract cash in exchange for forgiveness. They just want you to admit you need Jesus. I think I can do that."

"Really, Mom? Isn't that like joining in?"

"Yeah. It is. And I look at Betsy and Wayne—even your brothers and sisters—and I realize I want what they have. I want peace. I don't want to be so weary all the time." Mom set the spinning on the coffee table and stood. "I'm going to go for a walk."

Indigo's eyebrows lifted and she watched as her mom slipped into snow boots, dragged on a heavy coat, and bundled on a hat before disappearing through the door. That was abrupt. She checked the time. She'd give Mom an hour or so before she worried. It was clear and cold outside. Mom'd be fine. For all Indigo knew, Mom was heading to find Betsy and talk God.

She laughed.

That was probably exactly what Mom was doing.

Well, good for her. Indigo wasn't there yet, but she was willing to admit that it was different than she expected. And maybe it was something she'd think about.

For now? She was going to put Jesus and the forty dates she'd promised Joaquin out of her mind.

She picked up her mom's spindle and twisted.

Forty dates. What had she been thinking?

"MERRY CHRISTMAS, DARLING." Betsy pulled Indigo into a tight hug. As she eased back, she pressed a kiss to her cheek. "I'm so glad you're living here at the ranch now."

"Thanks. I am, too." Surprisingly, it wasn't just a polite lie. She really meant it.

The whole family—which included Joaquin, and Royal's girlfriend, Sophie—had attended the Christmas Eve service at the Hewitts' church the night before. If Indigo had ever been to a candlelight service before, she didn't remember. It had touched her.

She knew, sort of, the story of Mary and Joseph and baby Jesus. But this year, staring at the days and weeks ahead that would culminate in her giving birth to her own child, it was different.

"Hi, Wayne. Merry Christmas." Indigo smiled and hugged her grandfather.

"What's it going to take for you to decide to call me Grandpa like the rest of your siblings do?" Wayne winked.

"Oh. Um." Indigo looked away and spotted her sister Skye leaning against her husband's legs. Royal sat beside Sophie on the couch. Cyan had his stepson Calvin on his lap, while Maria, his wife, was bustling around in the kitchen. Did everyone really call him Grandpa? "I guess I can do that. I'm sorry."

"Don't be sorry. Betsy and I want you to be comfortable more than anything else." He took her hand and gave it a little tug. "Let's go and get a seat before all the good furniture is taken and we end up on the floor. It's one thing for you young people, but you get to be my age, and it's not as easy to get back up again."

Indigo laughed. Neither Wayne nor Betsy looked or acted their age. She and Wayne found two unoccupied arm chairs and sat. She watched the family laughing and her heart filled. This wasn't something she was used to. Her family had been close, living on the bus. But it had lacked something. It didn't seem to anymore. "Where's Mom?"

Cyan glanced over and gestured to the kitchen. "She's helping Maria. I couldn't convince her not to. And you know how Mom is. It's better not to fight when she gets that look in her eye."

That was true. "When do we give out the presents?"

Wayne laughed. "Soon. You and Calvin can hold it together just a few more minutes, okay?"

"Okay." She smiled. She wasn't expecting anything. She was excited to see what Wayne and Betsy thought of her gifts for them. She hadn't gone all out for her immediate family—that wasn't something they'd ever done—but she'd still thrown together either a hat and scarf or a pair of socks for everyone. After a little thought, she'd made socks for Joaquin, too. He was the father of her child. She probably owed him a Christmas gift.

Indigo swallowed. Father of her child.

"Honey, why don't you read us Luke chapter two." Betsy handed Wayne a Bible before finding a seat.

Wayne flipped to the right page, cleared his throat, and began. "In those days, a decree went out . . ."

Indigo listened, even though they'd read the same passage at church the night before. She'd even looked it up on her app when she'd been in bed and unable to sleep. Could it really be true? It seemed so hard to believe, and yet something in her yearned to be able to.

When Wayne set the Bible aside, he glanced her way with a soft smile, then turned to Calvin. "I believe, young man, that you asked to play Santa. So get to it."

"Yay!" Calvin jumped off Cyan's lap and dove under the tree. He snatched a pile of presents, read the tags, and spun around the room to put them in the correct recipient's lap. When everyone had something, he grabbed a big box and dragged it over close to Cyan.

"Do we go one at a time? Or all at once?" Indigo leaned toward Wayne. Her gift sat in his lap.

"All at once, mostly."

As if those words were the starting pistol, the sound of crinkling and tearing paper filled the air. Indigo watched as Betsy neatly slid her finger under the tape and carefully peeled away the paper to reveal the deep purple cardigan.

"Oh." Betsy lifted the garment and stroked it against her face. "Ohh. This is too much, Indigo. It's so lovely."

Indigo beamed. "It's a new pattern I'm working on."

"You designed this, too?" Betsy's eyebrows lifted, and she held it out in front of herself, admiring it. "You're a woman of many talents. I'm putting it on right now."

There was nothing better than seeing someone immediately appreciate your gift. Betsy shrugged out of the cardigan she had over a turtleneck and slipped her arms into the sweater from Indigo. Again, she stroked the sleeve against her cheek.

"Does it fit all right? I had to guess."

"It's perfect. I love it, thank you." Betsy stood and wrapped Indigo in a tight hug.

Warmth spread through her, and she turned to Wayne. He was holding his sweater with tears in his eyes. "What's wrong?"

He blinked and shook his head. "I'm a sentimental fool. This is a real treat. It's so soft, too. Is it from your sheep or the alpacas?"

"That's alpaca. It's the natural color—I thought it was interesting the way it was."

He nodded. "Just like God made it. I love it. Thank you."

"Will you put it on so I can be sure it fits?"

"Of course." He chuckled and worked the sweater over his head.

Indigo frowned. The neck wasn't as roomy as she'd hoped, but the shoulders were in the right spot and it was a good length. She touched the collar. "Is this too snug? I could re-do it."

"No. It's fine. Just takes a little effort to get over my noggin.

It's because my brain's so big, you see."

Indigo laughed.

"Don't listen to him." Betsy chuckled. "His brain is exactly the same size as everyone else's. If we needed to, could we stretch it a little when it was damp rather than making you redo it?"

"Sure. Let me know though, I'd be happy to help."

"Are you going to open yours?" Betsy nodded to the package sitting in Indigo's lap.

"Oh. Of course." She looked at the scribbled information on the tag and her head jerked up.

Joaquin smiled and gave her a slight nod when their eyes met.

The cozy, warm feeling from watching her grandparents open their gifts took on a sizzling, electric edge. Joaquin had gotten her a gift. Were the socks she'd made for him enough? Too personal? Too impersonal? She ripped open the paper and looked at the envelope.

He'd wrapped a card?

"Open it." Joaquin called out just loud enough to be heard over the other chatter in the room as people discussed their gifts and Calvin brought around a new load for people.

Indigo flipped it over and lifted the flap. There had to be thirty pieces of paper in there. She reached in and pulled out the stack. Good for one foot rub. She flipped to the next. Good for one errand, any sort. She flipped through the rest. They were all coupons. The warmth spread but that hint of tingling electricity remained along the edges.

He was thoughtful. And kind.

It probably wasn't even a good idea—they were so different —but was there any possibility they could make something beyond co-parenting work? Indigo wasn't sure.

But a large part of her heart wanted to give it a try.

10

"You busy tonight?" Joaquin looked around the cottage Indigo was setting up as her yarn business. She'd been doing a lot. Shelves now lined one wall—where had they come from?—and yarn hung from pegs in—what were they called?

Indigo looked up from her spinning wheel. "Tonight?"

He nodded.

"It's New Year's Eve."

He nodded again.

She shrugged. "I hadn't thought about it. It's not like I'm going to go out partying."

He smiled. That was good. There'd been a part of him that wondered if she was one of those women who didn't see the need to change their habits during pregnancy. He hadn't quite figured out how to bring it up. "No. I get that. Not really a lot of that to be had here anyway, unless you wanted to drive to Santa Fe. But I thought it might be nice to do something to ring in the new year anyway. Low key, I promise."

"Is this one of the forty?"

"It can be." Was she going to hold him to that number? He'd

thought maybe they'd made more progress than that. "Are you keeping track?"

She laughed. The sound did something crazy to his insides, but he fought to keep it from showing. "No. Probably not. You're the one who put a number on it."

"I didn't want you to wiggle out of seeing me." And giving him a shot to be a dad. His lips curved. A dad. Maybe this wasn't quite how he pictured it, but the idea was growing on him. "Speaking of that—or, well, not really."

Indigo snorted. "Which is it?"

"One thing led to another in my brain." He shrugged. "You make a doctor appointment yet?"

"Ah. Yeah. I was going to text you the details. Monday, the sixth. At nine thirty."

He pulled out his phone and tapped his calendar so he could add the information. "You want to leave around nine?"

"That should be fine. It's in town, but it didn't look too bad on the mapping app."

It was maybe fifteen minutes into town from here. Leaving a little extra for paperwork or whatever was never wrong. "Nine should do. So, tonight?"

"Yeah, why not? It's not like I have better offers. What are we doing?"

"Do you ever play Xbox?"

"Seriously?" She set her hands in her lap and frowned at him. "That's your idea of a New Year's Eve date?"

He shoved his hands in his pockets. "Around here? Yeah. With a little more prep time, I guess I could've found something swanky in Santa Fe, but that's not my scene. And I don't actually think it's yours."

She blushed and looked away.

"Am I wrong?"

She looked back and sighed. "No. Not really."

"What does your usual New Year's Eve look like? Be honest."

Indigo groaned and gave her spinning wheel a push. Her feet moved on the pedal and her hands did something to add the fur to the string winding around the big wooden circle that spun on one end. "Most of the time? In bed by ten. Animals get you up no matter what day of the year it is."

"Sounds about right." He grinned. "So this should be more interesting. And maybe we'll even make it to the ball drop. You ever watch the big to-do in New York City?"

"Sometimes. It's not really all that interesting. A big crowd freezing their tails off together to listen to musicians I've never heard of." She moved her shoulders. Not quite a shrug, but close enough.

He couldn't disagree with her. On TV, there was the added bonus of commentators narrating every moment, so it wasn't like when he'd gone. "I went one year."

"To New York?" If he'd said he'd gone to the moon, Joaquin wasn't sure she would have sounded more surprised.

"To New York. Seemed like the thing to do at the time. It was before I came here—I lived on the East Coast so it wasn't as hard to get up there." His parents probably still went into the city every month or so for one reason or another. Mom would drag Dad to any Broadway performance she could get tickets for. Or the symphony. Dad liked the food. He was always game to try a new restaurant. Especially if they had an unusual ethnic food to offer.

"You lived on the East Coast."

"New Jersey, mostly. It's not all Newark and Jersey Shore. Most of the state has earned the nickname The Garden State. My parents are still there."

"Why didn't you go see them for the holidays?"

Joaquin perched on the arm of the sofa she'd arranged knit throws over. "When I started working here and became a Christian, they told me not to bother coming home until I was ready to grow up. They think I should quit playing rancher, quit bothering with Jesus, and figure out a way to get rich."

"You don't want to be rich?"

"Not really. I have everything I need here. And more than that, I figured out in high school that focusing on money never seemed to make my parents happy. The more Dad earned, the more they fought, and the more pressure he seemed to feel to go earn more, as if it was going to solve all their problems. I've been happier here with room and board and a little bit of spending money than I ever was growing up with my every wish handed to me." Not many people knew about his family. He'd told Tommy some of it. And Wayne. But he didn't want to dwell on it even still. "I call my mom once a month to check in and see how they're doing. The conversation is pretty much always the same."

Indigo had stopped spinning again and was frowning at him. "Do you love them?"

"Of course, I do."

She shook her head. "I don't think that's an 'of course' kind of question. I'm not sure I loved my dad."

"Is it that? Or are you still upset about Jade?"

She snorted. "I'm definitely still upset about Jade. Maybe that's coloring it. I don't know. How am I supposed to be a good mom when I come from all that weirdness? We grew up on a bus! And you've got this family you barely talk to. So it's not like you're any better off."

"I have a family. Sure, there's Mom and Dad. And our relationship isn't bad, it's just not warm. But I also have Betsy and Wayne. I have Tommy, who's like a brother. Morgan, too. Now Royal and Skye and Sophie." He waited until she met his gaze. "And you."

She looked away. "We're not family, Joaquin."

"Not yet. But we could be." Was that pushing too much? She

hadn't appreciated his offer to get married. It had admittedly been unromantic, but the impulse behind it was still there. He could easily fall in love with Indigo. Right now, that could be a horrible idea. She didn't believe in Jesus, and he'd never wanted to date someone who wasn't a Christian before. But she was softening to it. He'd seen that at church. So maybe? He needed to do more praying. "Anyway. Tonight. Xbox. Want to come to my place around six?"

"You're not going to pick me up?" Her eyes were laughing, even though she tried to keep her face serious.

He could play along. "All right, fine. I'll pick you up at six. I'll have food, so don't eat dinner."

"Even if I ate dinner, I'd still want food." She frowned. "You remember I'm vegan, right?"

"No one's likely to forget that." He held up a hand. "Not because you're obnoxious about it. Just because it does come up. And I've watched you eat. But I've taken that into consideration."

"Okay." She offered him a half-smile. "I guess I'll see you."

Joaquin took that as his cue and stood. He gestured to the wall of yarn. "I like what you're doing here. It's impressive."

Her cheeks pinked. "Thanks."

"Anytime." He strode to the door. There were still some chores to do before he could focus on getting ready for their date tonight. And something about the way she looked at him made him want to pull out all the stops.

When was the last time someone did something special for Indigo and made her feel loved?

By FIVE, Joaquin was in his cabin, frantically trying to follow the recipe Maria had emailed him. It shouldn't be this hard! They were instructions. He just had to follow them, one step at a time, and then, at the end, he'd have a vegan version of posole. Which basically meant it was a whole bunch of pinto beans, hominy, and some green chile, since he couldn't add the part he loved best: pork. Maria insisted that it tasted good—she'd been tweaking a recipe she found online since the weather started getting cooler—so he was going to run with it. Maybe the big bonus was that it went much faster, since he didn't have to worry about cooking the pork all the way through.

But still.

Joaquin dipped a spoon into the broth and tasted it. It was rich and tomatoey and close enough. He wasn't sure how spicy to make it. He loved a spicy posole—probably safer to err on the less spicy side. He could always toss a little extra chile into his bowl. Too bad he hadn't thought about making pork on the side for himself. At least Indigo didn't seem to be one of those vegans who pushed it on everyone. He didn't understand it, really, but she seemed content to coexist with carnivores, so he wasn't going to sweat it, either.

He covered the pot, checked that the heat was on low, and went to the list he'd set on the table. Joaquin crossed through where he'd written the word "dinner" and scanned what was left to do. Shower and tidy. Easy enough.

At a quarter to six, he was down to pacing the length of his living room. It took maybe a minute to walk over to the cabin where Indigo and her Mom were staying. He could go now and be early, but what message did that send? He was too eager. Anxious.

Plus he'd have to talk to Indigo's mom.

She seemed nice enough in the interactions they'd had, but Indigo had to have mentioned the baby. He closed his eyes. They were going to have to tell everyone. Soon. He mostly knew he wasn't going to get kicked off the ranch because of it. Or at least, that was his prayer.

He'd messed up. No question. But he was trying to do the right thing now. That had to count for something, didn't it?

Blowing out a breath, Joaquin strode to the door and wrenched it open. It was snowing. He reached for his jacket and shrugged it on. It wasn't a long walk, but there was no sense in getting wet.

Hands stuffed in his pockets, he headed for Indigo's place. He stomped up the steps, as much to let them know he was coming as to get the snow off his boots, and knocked.

Elise opened the door with a smile. "Hi, Joaquin. Come in out of the snow."

"Thanks." He stepped in. It was awkward already. He cleared his throat. "How are you doing tonight?"

"I'm well. Looking forward to heading up to the main house to spend the evening with Betsy and Wayne. They said something about card games and the TV."

Joaquin nodded. "They like gin rummy."

"At least I know how to play that." Elise gestured toward the living area. "Why don't you come in and sit down? Indigo's never been one who worried about being ready early."

"Oh." That was an interesting tidbit to file away. He followed Elise and perched on the edge of a cushion at the far end of the couch. "How are you settling in? Feel like home yet?"

Elise laughed. "I can be at home anywhere. That's a skill I picked up fairly early on in my relationship with Martin. Are you going to marry my daughter?"

Joaquin blinked. "I asked her. She said no."

Elise sighed. "It's probably my fault. Mine and Martin's. We never got married. You probably know all the sordid details."

"I don't know as I'd call them 'sordid.' The two of you raised a family together, and your children are good people. We're glad to have them at the ranch."

"Aren't you kind?" Elise shrugged and settled back in her

seat. "I want more than that for my kids. I balked at first with the weddings—it seemed so predictable. But now? Seeing the mess Martin left for me? They deserve more than what I got."

"So did you."

Elise reached over and squeezed his hand briefly. "Thank you. Don't give up on her. She gets her stubbornness from both of her parents. It's not going to be an easy road."

"Most things worth anything aren't." Joaquin smiled.

"You're early." Indigo padded into the room in leggings and a bright orange tunic-length sweater. The wide cowl neck showed off her collar bones and a gold heart locket nestled at the base of her throat. She sat in a chair and tugged on boots that reached her knees.

His mouth went dry. "You look nice."

"New Year's." Indigo lifted a shoulder. "Plus you said 'date.' Even if we're just playing Xbox."

Now Joaquin wished he'd figured something else to do. There were probably parties in town—the hotel surely had something going on. Some of the restaurants, too. But it was also probably too late. And he didn't want to go down the hill and be around a ton of people. He liked it here on the ranch. He liked the idea of a quiet, laid back evening where they could have fun and talk. Get to know more about each other.

And that posole smelled amazing.

"Are you ready?" He stood, then glanced at Elise. "Would you like me to run you down to the house? Or walk with you? The snow's coming down pretty well."

"Wayne's going to fetch me. I think I may stay down there, as well." Elise glanced at her daughter. "If that's all right."

"Of course. Have a good time, Mom." Indigo leaned in and kissed her mom on the cheek. She straightened and nodded to Joaquin. "Lead the way."

He held out his hand. Would she take it? Was it too much?

Indigo glanced down then back up at his face. He could practically hear her thinking. After what felt like an eternity, she slipped her hand in his.

Joaquin smiled and started for the door. "Let's see what New Year's holds."

11

Indigo tucked her hands in the pockets of her coat to keep from twisting her fingers together. She didn't, as a rule, bother with doctor visits. There were any number of reasons for that. She was healthy. Wingfeather hadn't been a fan, and it was easier to go along than to fight with him about it. And she was busy.

That all changed when there was a baby in the picture.

A baby.

She glanced over at Joaquin. He sat impossibly still on the seat beside her. He looked pale, too. Indigo leaned closer and whispered, "You okay?"

He nodded. "Still wrapping my head around this. You?"

"Yeah." She let out a breath. It was good to know she wasn't the only one struggling. "I'm not sure what to expect. I did some searching online, but still. I think maybe you should just wait out here until they do the ultrasound. Is that okay?"

"Whatever you want." Joaquin turned and held her gaze. "I'm just here to support you and the baby."

She melted. Even as she fought against it, Indigo couldn't

stop his words from seeping into her heart and warming her. Had anyone ever cared for her like that? If she had to ask, the answer was probably no.

"Indigo Hewitt?" The nurse stood in the doorway wearing hot pink scrubs and carrying a clipboard.

"That's me." Who else would it be? The waiting room was empty but for them. Indigo rested her hand on Joaquin's knee a moment before standing. "I'll make sure they come get you."

He nodded.

"Follow me this way, and we'll get your vitals."

Indigo tried to pay attention, but there was a low-grade buzzing in her ears. She was really here. At the doctor's office. For a pre-natal exam.

What kind of bizarro world did she live in that she could be with someone for years, desperately hoping for a child, and make one mistake with someone else and end up pregnant? The pastor never mentioned God's sense of humor in his sermons—or at least he hadn't yet—but Indigo was pretty convinced He had one.

She made it through the exam, listening as the doctor chatted about what to expect and the vitamins she needed to start taking. All the basic information she'd already looked up online.

The nurse knocked then wheeled in the ultrasound machine. "Let's get a look at this baby. You ready, Mama?"

Mama. Indigo shrank into herself. "My friend—the dad—is out in the waiting room. Can he be here for this part?"

The doctor's eyebrows lifted, but she nodded to the nurse.

Indigo kicked herself. She should have just said boyfriend. Or fiancé. Anything that would have made this situation more respectable. At least she hadn't gone so far as to say one-night stand. Friend with benefits? Even if those benefits had only ever happened one time.

Before she could spend much more time berating herself, Joaquin came in with the nurse. He moved to stand by her head and kept his eyes fixed on the screen of the ultrasound.

Indigo reached for his hand. His fingers were warm as they wove through hers and his grip was a comforting, grounding presence. She gasped as the cold gel squirted on her belly.

"Sorry. Is it cold? I guess the warmer's not working." The doctor glanced at the nurse who nodded. Whatever that was about. Maybe telling her to go look into it? "Listen."

A quiet whooshing filled the room.

"Is that the heartbeat?" Joaquin's voice was reverent.

The doctor grinned up at him. "It is. Let me take some measurements and print some photos for you. They're not amazing at this age, just to warn you."

Indigo nodded. She'd looked that up online, too. But that, at least, had been fascinating. There were ultrasound photos at practically every stage available online, and she'd been able to see the development of the baby as the weeks progressed. Now, that was going to happen inside her.

She squeezed Joaquin's hand.

He leaned over and kissed her forehead.

Indigo closed her eyes. He was a sweet man. Why would he stay, when he deserved so much better than this?

INDIGO HEFTED the box of shipping supplies out of the back of her truck and started toward what she'd started calling her fiber cabin. Hmm. She turned the words over in her head. That might actually make a good business name. The Fiber Cabin. It had potential, at least.

"Here, let me get that." Joaquin appeared from behind her

and plucked the box out of her arms like it didn't weigh anything. "Should you be carrying stuff like that?"

She scowled. "I'm pregnant, not an invalid. Women in some countries in Africa walk twenty miles a day for water and lug it back home while they're pregnant. I can carry a box."

"What's the infant mortality rate in Africa again?" Joaquin leaned against the doorjamb.

Indigo fumbled her keys out of her pocket, her scowl deepening. Who did he think he was, sauntering over here with his big muscles and acting like he had the right to boss her around? In the two weeks since her first doctor appointment, he'd been turning up more often. "You're like a bad penny."

He laughed. "No one says that anymore."

"Then how did you know what I meant."

He shrugged. "I like old movies."

"You?" She unlocked the cabin door and frowned at him. Old movies were not what she pictured him watching. Unless . . . "John Wayne, right?"

"Westerns? No. Ugh." Joaquin made a "yucky" face. "Gary Cooper. Fred Astaire. Gene Kelly. Danny Kaye. They knew what was what."

"Danny Kaye." Indigo pointed to the corner of the main room, where she'd put the box that came yesterday—all by herself without any trouble, for the record. "Put it there. You're telling me you watch musicals."

"Sure, what's not to love?" Joaquin set the box down before wandering to her yarn wall and reaching out to touch a bright orange skein of wool "Fancy costumes, catchy tunes, dames spinning around in full skirts that show off their legs. Musicals should be the national pastime, not baseball."

"Dames?" She laughed. "If you've ever used that word in an actual conversation that wasn't about musicals, then I think I understand why there aren't women beating down your door."

"Hey. I have options." Lightning fast, he took her in his arms and swept her into a fox trot—or at least that was what she thought it was. It was too fast for a waltz, which was the only dance step she knew—then spun her out. "I don't happen to be interested in any of them right now."

Indigo shook her hand loose and crossed her arms, fighting a smile. "Who are you, and what have you done with the sullen cowboy I know?"

He frowned. "I'm neither sullen nor a cowboy. Do you see any cows around here?"

"Fine, fine. I'll surrender on the cowboy front."

"I'm not sullen."

"Uh-huh."

"I'm a man of few words." Joaquin nodded once at the end for emphasis. "Once you get to know me, I'm a lot of fun."

That . . . was true. She had to give him that, too. Except this whole situation was just surreal.

"You don't believe me?"

She lifted a shoulder. Not because she didn't believe him. He'd just proved that he could be fun. It was more that she liked this flirty, teasing side of him. And she was starting to like who she was when that flirty, teasing guy was around.

"Wow." Joaquin clutched his heart. "That hurts. I guess I'll have to show you again."

Indigo backed away as he took a step toward her. What was he doing? She started to laugh as he reached out and grabbed her around the waist, his fingers digging into her ribs. "Stop! That's not fair!"

A throat cleared.

Joaquin turned and, since he was holding Indigo around the waist, she spun with him. She pushed his arm off and took a big step away.

"Sorry. Didn't meant to interrupt." Wayne's eyes were twinkling. "Betsy said I should come and see how your shop was coming together. Looks like it's maybe not just the shop."

"We're not—"

"She's not wrong." Joaquin frowned at Indigo and cocked his head to the side. "Were you about to say we're not together?"

Indigo hunched her shoulders. "Well, we aren't. Not in a traditional sense."

"Wow." Joaquin huffed out a breath. "I'll leave you to give Wayne the tour. But don't forget we have a date tonight, even though we're not together. I thought we could go into town for some Mexican. Text me if that doesn't suit. Otherwise, I'll pick you up at six."

Indigo watched him leave. He didn't stomp or slam the door, but disappointment and anger still vibrated off of his movements.

"You sure put your foot in that one." Wayne crossed the room and patted her shoulder. "I'd love the tour. But I also figured someone ought to let you know that we all know."

"You all know . . ." Indigo watched his face and heat crept up hers. "About the baby. Of course, you do. Because my mother wouldn't keep a secret if her life depended on it."

"To be fair to Elise, Betsy is pretty persuasive when she sniffs out secrets."

Indigo looked away. What did they think? Would they let her stay? Would they fire Joaquin? Her heart started racing. Could she have cost him his job?

Wayne's hand was on her shoulder again, heavy, warm, and comforting. "It's certainly not the order we'd want things to happen in, but we also wanted to make sure you knew it didn't change anything."

"It changes everything." Her eyes blurred as she stared at the corner where her spinning wheel sat. She sniffled and tried to battle back the tears before they could escape.

"Not everything." Wayne turned her shoulders and tugged her close. It was like being wrapped up in a teddy bear. "Doesn't change how much we love you. Doesn't change how much God loves you. And that's just for starters."

"Are you sure?" Her voice was muffled, her face nestled against Wayne's shoulder. She turned her head and kept her eyes closed. "I've been reading this Bible app. It has a lot to say about sin and how God can't stand it. I had to look up the word, but apparently 'fornication' is the fancy word the Bible uses for sex when you're not married. It plays into my current situation."

Wayne chuckled. "It does. But have you gotten to 1 John yet?"

She shook her head. She'd given up on the front-to-back reading method after Joaquin suggested Mark and John. She liked those better anyway. The stories of Jesus doing miracles and talking about the kingdom of heaven were interesting. She didn't always understand what Jesus was getting at, but she wanted to.

"Well, now. In 1 John, there's verse that goes, 'If we confess our sin, He is faithful and just to forgive us our sin and to cleanse of us all unrighteousness.' Sin doesn't have to define you. That's why Jesus died."

Indigo frowned. She'd glossed over that part at the end of the book of John. It was gruesome and so unfair. "It doesn't make sense."

"Not to us, no. But it did to God. In the Old Testament, God set up the system of sacrifice so that His people could confess their sin and be forgiven. It was a lot. Animals had to be brought to the temple and killed and offered to God in all different ways depending on what the person had done."

Indigo winced. Those poor animals. Bad enough that people wanted to eat them—but to just have to slaughter them? For a ceremony? Yuck. It was good that wasn't still happening today.

Wayne smiled slightly and continued, "Jesus made it easier.

He came to earth, died on the cross as a perfect sacrifice—not one that had to be redone over and over—and then God raised Jesus from the dead to show us that sin and death had been conquered. Now, instead of buying animals at the temple, all we have to do is accept what Jesus did on the cross for us to have our sins forgiven."

"It seems too easy. And then, what, He just forgives you over and over until you die? Why would He do that?" It seemed like that made Jesus a chump. And just thinking that didn't feel right. Not after everything she'd been hearing at church and reading in the Bible app.

Wayne sighed and gave her a squeeze. "He does forgive us. Over and over and over. The flip side though, which is even better, is that He gives us the Holy Spirit, who lives in us, and if we let Him, will help us change so that we don't sin as much or as often in the same ways as before. He transforms us into an image of Himself."

"That sounds hard."

This time, Wayne laughed. "It is. Loving Jesus isn't for wimps. And Indigo, I don't think you're a wimp. Now, I'm not going to push, so I'll leave it there unless you have questions."

"Not really. Not yet." There were questions jumbling around in her brain, but they didn't make sense. And if they didn't make sense to her, why would they make sense to her grandfather?

"All right. My door's open any time. Betsy's too. Even Joaquin."

She stepped back and studied her grandfather. "You're really not angry at him? It just sank in that I could have cost him his place here."

"A little disappointed, but no, not angry. And the only way he ever has to leave Hope Ranch is if he wants to. That's our policy for everyone." He smiled and turned to look at the wall of yarn.

"Show me around your operation here, would you? Looks to me like you're almost ready to open up for retail."

Indigo turned and studied the yarn wall. It was step one of about six thousand more that needed to be done before she'd be ready. But she was making progress every day, a little bit at a time.

Maybe that was all she could expect to do on any front.

12

J oaquin gently ran his hands down the sides of the ewe. She was definitely expecting. When he'd moved the sheep here, he and Indigo had talked about breeding and agreed to give everyone a year off. She'd wanted to be there to supervise—particularly with the alpacas, since it often required repeat breeding sessions for the animals to conceive.

"Joaquin!" Tommy waved from the other side of the gate.

"Hey, man. Come on in, just make sure it's latched behind you." Joaquin straightened and eyed the rest of the flock. Had he missed anyone else?

"What are you looking at?" Tommy stood beside Joaquin, thumbs hooked in his belt loops.

"We have a pregnant ewe. I'm trying to figure out if there are any others."

"How'd that happen?"

Joaquin snorted. "I was wondering that myself. We keep the rams separate. Obviously, someone got in. Maybe when we were finishing up their enclosures? I don't know."

"Just the one?"

"Think so. I'm kind of surprised Indigo hasn't noticed. She's in with the animals all the time, too. But this lady," Joaquin pointed to the ewe who was munching contentedly near Joaquin's feet, "has been hiding a lot. Now we know why."

Tommy laughed. "You up for a movie tonight?"

"Sure." There wasn't a lot else going on. He'd briefly considered the Wednesday service at church, but he didn't want to get roped into helping with the youth group again. The kids were fine, but there was Jennifer, too. She tended to be persistent. "What were you thinking?"

"I don't know. Something with a lot of explosions."

"Uh-oh."

"What?"

"Come on, Tom. You only want mindless violence when your ex is rattling the cage."

Tommy sighed. "Am I that predictable?"

"What's she doing?"

"I'm supposed to have Olivia out here for their spring break."

"And she said no."

"Her family booked everyone on a cruise. For the whole week."

Joaquin winced. Tommy was an example of the opposite of how he wanted things to work with Indigo. "You've got to take her to court."

"I just—why? Her dad is friends with two judges, I know he'd find a way for them to have the case."

"Which is illegal. Pretty sure."

Tommy shrugged. "Doesn't matter. They won't get caught. Who am I going to complain to? His best friend, the police chief?"

"There's that."

"Yeah." Tommy kicked at clod of dirt and sent it skittering. "I just want to see my daughter. Spend time with her. Make sure she knows her dad loves her. I'm pretty sure my ex tells Liv I don't."

"Also illegal."

Tommy held up his hands in a "what am I supposed to do" gesture. "Thing is, she's getting old enough now, she's going to have a say in custody if I did manage, somehow, to get my ex into court. And right now, if I had to guess? Mel—my ex—would make sure Olivia said she doesn't want to spend time with me. It's getting harder and harder to keep her for the full time Mel lets her go when I head up there. How long do I keep pushing?"

"Forever, man. She's your daughter."

"Mel's threatening to demand child support."

Joaquin laughed. "That's rich. She lives in her daddy's mansion. What on earth would she need your money for?"

"That's how she got Olivia away from me in the first place. If I went along with what Mel outlined, then she wouldn't make me pay. But now I'm rocking the boat."

"Seems to me, you're better off paying some and actually getting to see your daughter."

Tommy shot him a long look. "That's a point. I guess maybe I'll go call the lawyer I can't really afford."

"Then explosions."

Tommy nodded. "Then explosions. Pizza?"

"You think you can sweet talk them into delivery?"

"Probably. If I can't, I'll run down and get it. I'll let you know. Usual?"

Joaquin nodded, his mouth already starting to water for the pepperoni and green chile with extra cheese pie that only one place in town made. "I guess I better find Indigo and break the lamb news."

"Good luck with that. Although, seems only fair."

"What do you mean?"

"She sprung a pregnancy on you, now you get to spring one

on her." Tommy grinned and pointed a finger gun at him. "Later, man."

Joaquin snorted. Tommy was a real laugh riot when he wanted to be. He checked the time. It was almost four. She'd opened the shop for retail traffic officially on Monday. New month, new business was her thought. What were her hours, though?

He dusted his hands off on his jeans and headed toward the gate. He'd walk over there. If she was already closed up, he'd figure it out. Knowing her, though, she'd still be there even if she was closed to customers. She was doing a lot of spinning right now, working through her backlog of fleeces from last spring now that they were only a few months out from a new batch. She'd been putting off processing her own fiber so she had more time to take on clients—a guarantee of income, she'd said. Now she had time to work on her own.

Could he do anything to help her process them?

He'd ask.

He liked working with her. They were starting to find a routine. A rhythm. And their weekly dates added to it. He liked being with Indigo when they weren't working, too. Fact was, if she were a believer, he'd let go of his heart and just fall the rest of the way in love with her.

She came to church with him every week. That was progress. And Wayne said they'd had a couple of conversations. And Joaquin was praying every day—almost all day—for God to work this out.

Indigo had only had two doctor's visits so far. Apparently, she only needed one a month at this stage of things, but each one had made Joaquin more determined to be part of this baby's life.

One way or another.

The lights were still on in the cabin. He smiled and picked

up his pace, taking the two steps to the front door in one. The little painted sign on the door said "Open," so he turned the knob and walked in.

"Welcome to The Fiber—oh. It's you."

Joaquin laughed and closed the door. "What if I came here looking for some yarn? Is that any way to greet a potential customer?"

Indigo rolled her eyes and went back to spinning.

"How's it been going?"

"Eh. It's early days yet. The online sales have picked up. If I was banking on a retail store being my sole means of support, I'd probably be discouraged. But I'm not. In reality, I don't expect to do a lot of in-person business. We're kind of far from town for that."

He nodded.

"Is that why you came?"

"What? Oh. No. Do you want me to leave?" He tucked his hands in his pockets. "You're amazing. You know that, right?"

"What?" She stopped spinning, her mouth hanging open. "Where'd that come from?"

"In here." He tapped his chest, right over his heart. "I mean, look at you. You raise animals, shear them—"

"I don't do the shearing. I thought about learning, but it's a lot, and I'd only be doing it once a year, so I'd never really get good enough. I already booked one of the traveling companies. They'll be here March thirtieth."

"Isn't that the big ultrasound day?" He slipped his phone out of his back pocket and tapped the calendar. Scrolling a moment, he nodded and flipped it around. "That's the gender ultrasound."

"Oh. Shoot. I'll give them a call and see if we can shift a day on either side."

He frowned. "You didn't have it on your calendar?"

Indigo shrugged. "It's written down somewhere. And they remind me six different ways—at least one phone call, a text, an email—I think you'd have to die to be able to say you missed an appointment because you forgot."

That was only three ways, but he got her point. "Okay. Did you want me to call them? The shearers?"

"Nah. I know them. It shouldn't be a problem, especially since I'm asking so early. They're really only now starting to plan their route." She pushed the spinning wheel again to get it moving. "I know that isn't why you came."

"To compliment you? It might have been. And you didn't let me finish."

She shook her head.

She was grumpier than usual. He had to add that last part, because it seemed like there was always a tiny part of Indigo that held on to grumpiness like it was a security blanket. "Are you okay?"

Her eyes closed and she stopped the wheel again while she sighed. "I am. I'm just—this is all a lot. My jeans don't button anymore. I'm still behind on these fleeces but I'm already booking people to come give me more. I tried a new color combination and it's terrible. No one is going to buy that yarn. It's ugly. But what? I don't want to throw it out. That's like burning money. I'm overwhelmed."

Joaquin strode across the floor and stuck out his hand. "Stand up."

"What? No. Why?"

"Just stand up, and don't argue with me, okay?"

Huffing, Indigo set aside the roving and stood, arms crossed over her chest, her lips in a pout. "Happy?"

He chuckled and took her hand. He gave it a tug. She tugged away. Laughing, he tugged again, harder, and pulled her into his arms. He ran a hand up and down her back.

Indigo slowly relaxed against him. Her arms lowered and her hands settled at his hips. She laid her head on his shoulder. "I'm sorry I'm grumpy."

"I think you're entitled. You're growing a baby. On top of all the other amazing things you do. How have you been sleeping?"

"Ugh."

He smiled, his lips against her hair. He pressed a kiss to her forehead. All his protective instincts were on high alert. How could he help? He didn't know how to do anything with the fiber end of her business. He knew how to care for the animals—if she'd overlook whatever had happened that ended up with a pregnant ewe, who'd manage to escape notice until it was almost lambing time.

She sighed and her arms wrapped around his waist. "I didn't realize how much I needed a hug."

Joaquin tried to keep his voice light, but it still came out huskier than he intended. "Always happy to oblige."

She tilted her face up and met his gaze. "Are you sure you don't watch Westerns?"

He couldn't stop looking at her full, pink lips. Had she put something on them today? They had a shine he didn't usually notice. Of course, he usually managed to keep himself from staring at them, because that way lay madness.

Would it be so bad? One taste. Just one, simple kiss. Even a chaste one would be better than the torture of not kissing her.

Joaquin swallowed and dragged his gaze away from her lips.

"Why did you come, Joaquin?" Her voice was strained. Was it possible she felt it, too?

He peeked at her lips just as her tongue darted between them and her hands moved and began to slide up his chest. He bit back a groan and pulled her closer, staring over her head and away from those lips. He cleared his throat. "Um."

"You must have had a reason." Her lips pressed against the

side of his throat near his collar. Then again a little higher, just below his jaw.

Oh, man. Joaquin clenched his teeth together and focused on not giving in to the temptation to kiss her. He should let her go. Step back. Step away. He glanced at her and lowered his head. Closer. Just a little closer.

Would it be so bad?

"Was this why you came?" Her breath was warm and minty on his face.

"No. But it sure is nice."

"You're sure?"

"I'm sure. One of the ewes is pregnant. That's why I came. But I—"

Her hands pushed against his shoulders hard enough that he stumbled a half step back. "What?"

Joaquin blinked. Where before her face had been soft and dreamy, now there was fire. He held up his hands. "I don't know what happened."

"Really?" Indigo gestured to the tiny bump in her abdomen. "I think you understand how the process works. It's the same for sheep as it is for people. Didn't we agree to keep the rams separate?"

"We did. I did. It's just the one."

She shook her head and turned away. "This is just great."

"At the risk of you walloping me again, can I ask why it's bad? I know it's not what we'd planned, but sometimes it turns out okay. Right?" Would she figure out that he was asking about more than the sheep?

She turned back to him and sighed. "You're sure it's just one?"

"Pretty sure."

"I'll go out and look tomorrow. It's information I need for the shearers—we want them to come before she lambs. And you better read up on lambing, because I don't think I'm going to be in the best shape for that in two more months. Usually it goes fine and they don't need help, but sometimes not so much." She stepped closer and gently touched his shoulder. "I'm sorry I pushed you."

Joaquin shrugged. "I've had worse."

"Are you busy tonight?" She held out her hand. Was it part of the apology?

He took it, but nodded. And maybe it was for the best. "Already planning to hang with Tommy."

She waited a beat, and then nodded. "But we're still on for Friday."

"Do you want to be?"

"I do."

He smiled and some of the chill from her flash of anger faded. "Then we are. Can I meet you in the sheep pen tomorrow? I'd like to know what to look for. I'm sorry I missed this— all of it."

"It happens. And I didn't pick up on it, either." She leaned up and kissed his cheek. "Go play with your friend. I'll see you tomorrow."

He squeezed her hand and left the cabin, trying to decide if he was disappointed or relieved that they hadn't kissed. Either way, he wasn't going to be sleeping very well tonight.

13

"Is that what you're wearing?" Mom frowned at Indigo as she walked from her bedroom into the living room. "It's Valentine's Day, sweetie. You should dress up a little."

"Mom." Indigo shook her head. "It's not a date."

"Yes, it is. That's even the exact word he used when he asked you to dinner. A date. For Valentine's Day. In Santa Fe. Seems to me, if you're driving close to ninety minutes for a fancy dinner, you should dress up a little."

Indigo groaned. Her mom was making some good points. And yes, she'd agreed to forty dates with Joaquin in a moment of insanity. This was date number seven. That didn't count all the times they saw each other during the week or at church on Sundays. Joaquin had been very clear those didn't count toward the ridiculous number he'd suggested. Since they hadn't started the minute she got pregnant, forty was going to take them past the baby's birth. "Fine. Leggings and a big sweater are the most comfortable thing I own, though."

"Don't you have any dresses that are loose around the waist?" Mom stood and walked toward her bedroom. "Come on. I'll help you find something."

Dragging her feet, Indigo followed. They weren't going to find anything. Fancy clothes simply weren't part of her life choices. She had some flowing gypsy skirts and peasant blouses, but those didn't seem any more suited to fancy dinners in the city than leggings and a sweater. Or she had the dress she'd worn to Skye's wedding, but that was unlikely to still fit. Aside from the clothing problems, it had been nearly two weeks since they'd had that moment in the fiber cabin and he hadn't made any other moves to kiss her. It was confusing. And annoying. "Maybe I should cancel."

"No, you should not." Mom eyed the meager contents of Indigo's closet. "How did I raise daughters who don't love clothes? Your sisters are all like this, too. Azure paints things on overalls and considers that dressed up. You've got this mess. I don't think I've seen Skye in anything but jeans and a T-shirt since high school."

"She wore a very pretty dress at her wedding."

Mom shot her a look. "Weddings don't count. Azure even managed something sort of traditional for hers—even if it had splashes of color."

"I loved her dress. It was very Azure."

Mom laughed. "Yeah, it was. And Matt seems to suit her down to the ground. It's good to have kids I don't have to worry about."

"Meaning you have some you do worry about? Which would be me?"

Mom sank onto the edge of Indigo's bed. "Not really. The baby coming is a bit of a surprise, but I'm hardly one to throw stones at that. I lived with your father for a lot of years, had a lot of babies, and was never married. Joaquin seems like a good man who'll stick by you. And I guess I don't understand why you're pushing him away."

Was she pushing him away? Maybe she was. But everybody

left at some point. Having a little bit of control over it felt safer. Would her mother understand that? "I'm not *trying* to."

"Are you trying to keep him?" Mom closed her eyes and waved her hand. "Don't answer that. It's between you and Joaquin. Just know I like him. And a lot of why I like him is I see the way he is with you—the way he watches you when you aren't looking. He's teetering on the edge of being in love with you, and that's not something to take lightly."

Love? Did Indigo even know what that looked like anymore? Or felt like? How long had it been since she'd been able to believe Wingfeather felt anything for her beyond mild annoyance? "I . . ."

"Just think about it." Mom stood and scowled in the direction of Indigo's closet. "You don't have anything that's going to work. Let's go look at my wardrobe. Now that you've put on a few pounds, I might have something that fits better anyway."

Indigo's eyebrows lifted.

Mom snorted. "They're not all old lady clothes. Come on."

"You're not an old lady, Mom."

"Sure, I am." Mom shrugged. "It is what it is. We all get there, one day at a time, whether or not we want to."

Indigo stepped into her mom's room. She tried hard not to do that—it was better for them both to have a private space. She'd worried about sharing a cabin with Mom. Indigo had been on her own so long, she wasn't sure she remembered how to live with someone. Wingfeather didn't count. He was gone more than he was around—even in the early days. Mom had ended up being surprisingly easy to live with, though.

"Now, let's see." Mom slid a section of clothes aside and started eyeing dresses one at a time. "Oh. Let's try this."

Indigo studied the simple purple sheath dress. "It's going to show the baby."

"So what?" Mom pushed the hanger into Indigo's hands. "Go try it on. If you hate it, I'll keep looking."

Indigo set the dress on Mom's bed and stripped off her sweater. She slipped the dress on over her head and reached for the zipper.

"Let me do that." Mom moved around behind and tugged the zipper up. "Is it too snug?"

Indigo sat on the bed then stood and moved around. "No. I think it's okay. How does it look?"

Mom stepped back. Her eyes were shiny. "You're beautiful."

"Mom." Indigo cocked her head to the side. "What's wrong?"

She shook her head. "It's nothing. I'm okay."

"You're not."

"You're my last baby. I want to see everyone settled and happy. I never did feel you'd get there with Wingfeather."

"Why didn't you say something?"

Mom shrugged. "Who was I to interfere? Your dad and I raised you to know your own minds."

"We still all valued your opinions. I know that made it harder for Azure and Skye, in particular, when they started this whole Jesus thing."

Mom bit her lip. "About that."

Indigo closed her eyes. "You, too?"

"Yeah. Are you mad?"

"No. No, Mom, I'm not mad." She sighed and looked down at her legs. "It seems inevitable around here. I can't wear leggings with this. Or flats. Would my knee boots work?"

"I think they'd be great. And very you. Are you thinking about the Jesus thing?"

Indigo stopped in Mom's doorway and turned to meet her gaze. "A little, yeah."

"That's good, then." At the knock on the door, Mom startled. "You go get shoes, I'll let Joaquin in."

Indigo hurried to her room to finish getting ready. She heard Mom greeting Joaquin, but couldn't quite catch his response. Whatever he said must've been amusing though, since Mom's laughter carried loud and strong back into Indigo's bedroom. She smiled. It was good to hear Mom laugh. She'd seemed lighter the last week or so too. Was that because of God?

She looked at herself in the mirror and before she could talk herself out of it, turned to the side. Her belly was poking out. Not in the "Wow! You must be due any day!" kind of way, but she was obviously either pregnant or incapable of controlling how many cheese puffs she ate every day.

Her mouth watered.

The doctor had said she might crave meat and dairy during pregnancy. She'd also said Indigo shouldn't fight the cravings too hard, since it could be her body's way of letting her know the baby needed nutrients he or she wasn't getting from vegan choices. Indigo was fairly certain the ice cream and, yes, cheese puffs she'd been sneaking weren't what the doctor had meant.

Indigo grabbed her clutch and hurried into the living room. She halted abruptly when she spied Joaquin. "Wow."

Joaquin looked up, laughter in his eyes. The light turned from humor to elemental hunger in a flash.

Indigo swallowed. The dark grey suit with a turquoise bolo instead of the traditional tie was very Joaquin. The shiny pointed toes of black cowboy boots completed the image of Southwestern man out on the town. "You look good."

"I think that's my line. Though I might choose amazing."

Mom practically beamed from the couch. "I think I left something in my bedroom. You two have fun."

Joaquin straightened. "Are you sure we can't bring you something?"

"I am. Thank you, Joaquin." Mom squeezed Indigo's hand as she passed on the way to the bedrooms.

"Ready to go?"

Indigo nodded. A sudden awkwardness settled in her belly. "Yeah. Yes."

He offered his elbow. "Happy Valentine's Day."

"Thanks. Um. You, too." Indigo cringed inwardly. You, too? Could she say that? Lame. She cleared her throat as they exited the cabin and made their way to his truck. "You never did say where we were headed in Santa Fe."

"Nope." He held open the truck door for her, then closed it when she'd settled on the seat.

She frowned as he walked around the front of the cab and climbed in behind the wheel. "Are you not going to?"

"Don't like surprises?"

"They're okay, I guess." She looked out the side window as the engine rumbled to life and they started down the driveway to the mountain road. "It's so pretty. Sometimes it just catches me right here." She thumped her chest.

"I know the feeling."

The smile he sent her shot straight to her heart. Was he talking about the landscape? It seemed like he might also mean something else—something more. It occurred to her that she didn't mind nearly as much as she probably should.

INDIGO SHIFTED on the chair and tried to focus on the pastor as he launched into the first anecdote that he'd use to lead in the sermon. They were always interesting. Sometimes funny. Or at least groan-worthy in terms of a pun. She shifted again.

"You okay?" Joaquin's whisper tickled her ear.

She shivered. He shouldn't have this effect on her. But he did. It was just chemistry. Right? She turned. His face was right there. Her lips warmed and her gaze darted to his mouth then back to his eyes. She was *not* thinking about kissing him in church.

Oh, boy, yes, she was.

But she wouldn't follow through. She wasn't going to be the one who started their first real kiss. Or, well, their first real kiss since November. If he wasn't going to make a move, she wasn't either, no matter how much she wanted to. Indigo angled so she could whisper in his ear. "Just a fluttery feeling. It's not unpleasant. Just strange."

He nodded and took her hand.

It was comforting, so she wove her fingers through his and turned her attention back to the pastor. She used her left hand to scroll to the Bible passage on her phone. She was getting better at knowing where things were now—maybe it was time to take the church up on their offer of a physical Bible. Would it be different, somehow, to read it that way? Better? It might make taking notes easier. There were passages she'd read that she'd highlighted in the app, but then she couldn't find them later when she wanted to look at them again. There was no way—or at least no way she'd found—to see a list of all her highlighted passages. With an actual book, she could at least flip pages and look for them that way.

There was that fluttering again. What could it—her eyes widened.

Hand shaking slightly, Indigo rubbed her belly. The fluttering stopped. The baby. She could feel the baby.

Her eyes filled and she nudged Joaquin with her elbow.

He turned her way, and a hint of panic hit his face. "What is it? Are you sick?"

"Shhh." The woman behind them frowned at him.

Indigo hunched her shoulders as she shook her head and pulled her hand free from his. She opened a new text and tapped a message.

I THINK IT'S THE BABY. I THINK I FELT IT MOVE.

Joaquin's phone buzzed. He read the message and turned to her with a huge grin. He put his arm around her shoulders and tugged her closer. His lips brushed over her hair.

Indigo blinked back tears. Darn hormones. She rested her head on Joaquin's shoulder and switched back to her Bible app. *I feel you, baby. I'm going to be the best mom I can. I promise. And your dad?* Indigo swallowed and peered up at Joaquin through her eyelashes. *He's going to be amazing. You're lucky to have him. So am I.*

Joaquin was a good man. She was definitely lucky. Or, maybe her mom had it right—she'd switched to saying blessed all the time. Indigo wasn't sure she saw the difference, except . . . maybe she did.

She'd given Joaquin so many opportunities to leave. Wingfeather would have taken them. Oh sure, he'd come back eventually, but when it came to Wingfeather, an opportunity to leave was always something to seize.

Joaquin was the opposite. In the month since Valentine's Day he'd shown her over and over again. He didn't just stay. He pursued.

Maybe it was time to stop running.

14

"A girl?" Indigo looked away from the nurse and glanced up at Joaquin. Her gaze locked with his.

His heart thundered in his chest. A girl. He grinned. "I hope she's pretty like her mama."

Indigo blushed. "You're not disappointed?"

"Why would I be? Girls are special." A boy would be special, too, but there was time for that down the road. If he could convince Indigo to marry him and start a family. He hadn't given up on that idea—it was changing, slowly, into a dream that he actively craved rather than what seemed like something he should do—but the end result was still the same. He'd be a father to his child, and Indigo would stay part of his life.

"Here are your printouts." The nurse smiled and offered a short stack of grainy ultrasound images to Joaquin. "Make sure you stop at the front to schedule your next appointment before you go."

"I can, uh, leave you to get put back together." Joaquin couldn't tear his eyes from the black and white photos in his hand. "A girl. We need to start talking about names."

"Names." Indigo scooted to a sitting position. "You're serious."

"Of course I am. I told you before, I want this baby. I want to be part of her life. I'm her daddy." Joaquin fought back the surge of anger her words brought on. It wasn't going to help anything. Had they really made so little progress?

Indigo nodded. "I guess I didn't realize you meant it. Not really. Wingfeather—"

"Don't judge me by his broken yardstick."

Indigo snickered.

"I'm serious about that, too. I'm not him. I'm not walking away." He glanced at the door. "I'll wait for you in the lobby."

He clicked the exam room door shut behind him. She still expected him to leave? If he ever got his hands on Wingnut, he'd ... well, violence wasn't his go-to response, but he'd be sorely tempted to make an exception. Why did she cling to her experiences with him as some sort of representative sample of how all men were?

Her father was another piece of work. Or he had been. No one seemed all that upset that he was gone now. Maybe Elise— although he hadn't noticed Indigo's mom seeming particularly distraught. Probably the discovery of an illegitimate daughter a year ago had dulled some of the responses.

It all served to form Indigo's expectations though, didn't it? He nodded to himself. Well, he was going to stick. He already loved this baby girl and he hadn't met her yet. Just seeing the sweet bump of Indigo's belly could set him daydreaming about the future. And every minute he got to spend with Indigo pushed him closer to loving her.

He was holding back some—or trying to—because she still wasn't sure about Jesus. Wayne had had some good talks with her. And now Elise was a believer. Indigo was surrounded. Surely it was just a matter of time?

Indigo shuffled through the door into the lobby and shot him a tentative smile before she moved to the reception window to make her next appointment. She took the reminder card and turned. "Ready?"

Joaquin nodded and offered his hand.

Indigo studied it like it was a new species of insect before finally reaching out to weave her fingers through his.

"You want to grab some lunch?" He hadn't been able to eat his breakfast. The gender portion of the ultrasound was less important to him than all the other checks they'd done. Part of him wanted to say a healthy baby was all that mattered, but the reality was, he'd love her even if she wasn't. There'd be more preparation to do if they were looking at a child with physical challenges, but Joaquin was all in, whatever God chose to give them. Now, though, with the appointment behind them and reassurances that everything looked like it was going along just as it should be, he was starving.

"I could eat. I can always eat." Indigo chuckled as they left the building. "And Mom said she was happy to mind the store for as long as I needed. Not that I'm expecting a ton of traffic."

"You've only been open two months." Was she worried about that? "Did you expect something different?"

"Not really." Indigo squeezed his hand before letting go and climbing into his truck when he opened the door for her.

Joaquin closed the door and went around to the driver's side. "Can you do spicy?"

She nodded. "So far. You thinking the Cantina?"

"I was. That all right?"

"Yeah. Definitely."

A handful of minutes ticked by as he drove away from the doctor's office and headed toward what he and most of the folks at Hope Ranch considered the best restaurant in town.

"You're really not disappointed she's a girl?" Indigo's gaze was nearly palpable.

"I'm really not." He kept his eyes on the road, even though he wanted to look over and try to guess what she was thinking. "Should I be?"

"No. I don't want that. I just keep expecting you to give up."

His laugh held no mirth. "I'm aware."

"I'm sorry. I'm going to stop doing that. This thing we have between us—it's more than chemistry, isn't it?"

Now he did glance over. "It is."

"Okay." She took a deep breath and let it out slowly. "Okay. Thank you."

"For what?"

"Not giving up."

"Then you're welcome. Giving up's not my style. I'm in this, Indigo, for the long haul. You know what I want."

"I—no. I don't. What do you want, Joaquin?"

How did she not get it? He frowned and shook his head. "You. This baby. More children, down the road. A life together."

"You proposed because of the baby. Not because you loved me or wanted any of this." She turned and stared out her window.

"Initially, sure, but we've been out on fourteen dates. One a week for fourteen weeks. And that doesn't count all the times we've hung out and worked together in between, or the weeks before we started dating when you lived on the ranch, or the year you and I spent talking and emailing about livestock. I considered you a friend of sorts before you ever came to New Mexico. I realized the potential for me the minute you showed up." He winced. And then he'd acted on that initial chemistry and set this whole messy ball rolling because he hadn't stepped back and thought it through. "Maybe our relationship got started the wrong way, but I believe God can redeem it."

"That does seem to be His specialty." Her words were quiet.

Had he heard her right? The sliver of hope in his heart that kept him hanging on and praying for her salvation widened. He said a quick, mental prayer of thanks and begged God to keep him from messing it up. He didn't want to push and end up with a relationship that kept Indigo from deciding not to pursue God first.

Joaquin cleared his throat. "Have you given that any thought on a personal level?"

She laughed. "Yeah. I have. It'd be impossible not to at Hope Ranch. Between my grandparents and my mom, let alone Cyan and Maria and Skye and Morgan, even Calvin. There's really no other choice."

"Can I ask what's stopping you?"

"Stubbornness." Indigo shrugged. "If I boil it all down, it's stubbornness. Dad was so opposed to all of this. And it's not like he's some shining paragon of awesome, I know that. If I didn't, this whole situation with Jade would have proven it. But I can't help feeling like it's one final betrayal to give in and say, 'Nope, Dad, you were wrong about it all.' Even if he was."

"Have you heard from Jade?" Maybe it was better to pivot and turn the conversation away for now. He wasn't sure. But he really didn't want to bungle anything.

Indigo laughed. "No. Skye has. They text, I guess. Or Skye texts her and Jade gets back to her eventually. Jade still feels like we're all holding out on her inheritance."

"Seriously?" From what he understood, the kids had agreed to split everything from their father evenly with this new sibling. And then they'd all turned around and given it back to Elise. Except Jade, of course. She'd kept every penny.

Indigo shrugged. "Some people care more about money than anything else."

"That's true. Tommy's ex is like that." And Tommy's ex was

one of the reasons Joaquin was determined to make it clear to Indigo that she wasn't shaking him off. He could manage his own heartbreak, but he wasn't going to ask his child to do that, too. "All you can do is pray for them."

"That's what Skye says. Do you really believe it works?"

"What? Prayer? Yeah, I do." Joaquin turned into a parking spot near the door of the restaurant. "It doesn't always feel like it in the moment, but when you stop and look back over things? Prayer works. If it doesn't change the situation, it changes my heart and helps me cope with whatever is going on."

"I wish I had that confidence."

Joaquin reached across and took her hand. "It comes with practice."

"And the first step . . ."

"Is to believe." Joaquin held her gaze.

After a moment, Indigo looked down at their twined fingers. "If I'm honest, I already do. How do I make it official?"

Joaquin swallowed the lump in his throat. Did he really get to be with her when she took this step? "It's a simple prayer."

"Can you tell me what to say?"

"Sure. I can give you the gist—they're not magic words, though. You just admit that you're a sinner and say you're sorry, acknowledge that you believe that Jesus is the Son of God who died on the cross for your sins and was raised on the third day, and then ask Him to be your savior."

"I can do that. Do we have to be at church?"

"Nope. We can do it here."

"Right now?"

He waited until she looked up. "Why wait?"

Indigo squeezed his hand and closed her eyes. She prayed a stumbling, simple, prayer, before looking up at him with shining eyes. "Like that?"

He nodded and leaned across the console. He cupped her face in his hands, his eyes searching hers. "Just like that."

Before she could respond, he drew her closer and lowered his mouth to hers. There was no reason to hold back. Not anymore. Now she was everything—or she could be. Joaquin poured his heart into the kiss, giving himself over to the sensations that flowed through him.

Indigo groaned quietly.

Joaquin eased back. "We should go in and eat."

"Right."

"I love you, Indigo."

Her eyes widened.

He put a finger over her lips. "I've been wanting to say that for a while. You don't have to say anything. I just figured maybe you should know."

"Okay."

He chuckled and worked to keep his tone light. He couldn't give in to the aching need to kiss her again. Not yet. They should go in, get some food.

At least that would feed some of the hunger that raged inside him.

"So? How'd it go?" Tommy propped his feet on Joaquin's coffee table and reached for his Xbox controller.

"Good. It's a girl."

"Yeah? Congrats, man. She going to keep letting you be part of things?"

Joaquin reached for his controller and tried to keep his thoughts from returning to their kiss in the cab of his truck. Or the one on her porch when he'd dropped her back at the fiber cabin. Or the one in the equipment shed when she'd stopped by to check on the pregnant ewe, and he'd been in there checking on feed levels.

"You in there?" Tommy's elbow collided with Joaquin's.

"Sorry. I am. And I think so. Things are moving in the right direction, I think."

Tommy turned to look at him.

Heat crawled up Joaquin's neck. He was saved by a knock at the door. "That should be Royal."

"He's coming here?" Tommy dropped his feet from the table and shifted over to a separate chair.

"Come on in." Joaquin closed the door behind Royal and eyed the bag of chips in his hand. "Those for us?"

"Figured snacks were always good." Royal headed into the living room.

"No Sophie tonight?" Tommy's voice held a hint of scorn.

Royal sent him a cool look. "She had something with her mom and sister—wedding stuff."

"You engaged yet?" Tommy scrolled through the game options on Joaquin's display and frowned. "Is this TV going to be big enough for a three-way split screen?"

"We've done it before. What's the problem?" Joaquin dropped onto the sofa beside Royal.

"Yeah, what's going on?"

Tommy jerked a shoulder. "Nothing. Just asking a question."

"To go back, no, I haven't proposed to Sophie yet. I was thinking maybe at Easter. That'd be six months."

"That's in like two weeks." Joaquin clicked on the first-person shooter they all enjoyed and started it loading. "You know that, right?"

Royal paled. "I knew it was in April."

Tommy laughed.

Joaquin chuckled. "You're not wrong. But two weeks. Do you have a ring yet?"

"Not yet. I guess I need to go shopping. I'll look around online tonight. Morgan got Skye's ring online, I think. I could ask him where."

"With two weeks to go, I'm not sure online shopping is going to get you the results you need." Tommy shook his head. "You need to go to Santa Fe. You doing the traditional diamond or does she prefer something else? Do you know her ring size?"

Royal blinked.

"You don't know?" Tommy snorted. "Maybe you ought to wait a little longer, son."

"Hey. I can figure it out. And I do know her ring size, for the record. Her sister borrowed a ring from Sophie not too long ago so I could get it measured." Royal hit a button and joined the game. "What's wrong with you tonight, Tommy? Something's up."

Tommy sighed. His head dropped back and he closed his eyes.

"Problems with the ex," Joaquin muttered and reached for the bag of chips. If that was the case, all this talk of weddings and babies was probably what had set him on edge.

"Got it in one." Tommy shook his head and leaned forward, propping his elbows on his knees. "My lawyer reached out to hers to see about enforcing our current custody agreement. The answer was basically that I could push it, if I wanted, but we'd end up back in court. I don't know what to do. I just want my daughter to know me. And to know I love her."

Dread settled in the pit of Joaquin's stomach. He couldn't let that happen to his kid. Not that Tommy had set out to have it happen to him—but what would it take to get Indigo to marry him? He didn't think she'd end up like Tommy's ex—that woman was pure evil—but any extra protection would be a good thing.

"Sorry, man." Royal reached over and gave Tommy's shoulder a light punch. "Are we playing, or what?"

Joaquin laughed. Leave it to Royal to shift the mood. "Yeah, let's do this."

Tommy nodded and hit a button on his controller.

"I ran into my sister this afternoon." Royal maneuvered his character away from the spawn point and started clicking on lockers full of weapons and ammo.

"Which one, man? It's not like that's helpful." Tommy zipped his character off in a different direction, already firing at the little worm-like creatures popping up out of the sand.

"Indigo. Sorry. Figured she was the only one a certain someone would care to hear about." Royal glanced at Joaquin with his eyebrows raised.

"I like both your sisters." Joaquin swapped out weapons and ran to join Tommy in the battle.

"Uh-huh. She mentioned the two of you had lunch after the doctor's appointment. Hey—save me some bad guys!" Royal finally moved away from the spawn point and ran into the fight.

Joaquin concentrated on shooting things. What part had Indigo mentioned?

"If you've got dirt, you need to spill it. Joaquin over there is busy ignoring you, man." Tommy laughed. "And now I'm curious about lunch. All he told me was that the baby's a girl."

"It is? She is?" Royal let out a whoop. "Indigo didn't mention that part. Maybe she didn't get around to it because everyone got rowdy when she told us she'd asked Jesus to be her savior."

"Yeah? Cool. I guess Wayne and Betsy were there?" Tommy hit his controller buttons furiously then groaned as his character disintegrated into sparkling squares. "Aw, man."

"And Mom and Cyan and Maria and Calvin and Skye and Morgan."

Joaquin nodded. Indigo had invited him to the family

dinner, but he'd passed. It hadn't seemed like something he should be part of. Yet. Maybe he should have said yes?

"Thanks, Joaquin."

Joaquin frowned at Royal. "For what? I didn't do anything."

"Well. I mean, you helped her get there."

Joaquin shook his head. "Nah. That's all God. I was in the right place at the right time."

Royal shrugged. "I'm still glad. A girl, huh? Have any name thoughts?"

"Not yet. I guess we need to talk about the whole family 'blue' thing. Is she going to want to carry that on?" Did she need to? There were a lot of things he and Indigo still needed to talk about now that they were making some progress in their relationship.

15

I ndigo stood at the fence rail and watched as the shearers worked their way through the alpaca herd. The first time she'd seen it done, she'd been concerned—it looked like it should hurt, or be dangerous—but it wasn't, and losing their fleece was necessary for the health of the animals.

Greg, the older of the shearers, finished running the clippers down Captain Janeway's leg before nodding to the young man helping him. He released the ropes and got out of the way as Janeway wiggled to her feet and sprinted off the shearing mat.

Indigo grinned. "Looks good."

Greg gave her a snappy salute before gesturing for his helper to bring on the next animal. "Just two more, looks like, and we'll move on to the sheep. Sure you don't want to give it a shot and learn how to do your own herds?"

"Positive." Indigo pressed her hands into her back. "You make it look easy. I know it isn't."

Greg laughed. "All right. Have to ask."

Movement at the corner of her eye had Indigo glancing over. She brightened. Joaquin walked toward her. His long, leggy gait made her mouth water. It shouldn't be legal for someone to look that good in faded jeans.

"Hi." Joaquin brushed his lips across hers and slid his hand to the small of her back. "How's it going?"

"So far so good. Almost done with the alpacas."

Joaquin looked out at the setup and nodded. "They're fast."

She laughed. "They're professionals."

"You mom invited me to dinner tonight."

Indigo's eyebrows lifted. "She did? That should be fun."

"Did you want me to say no?"

She glanced up at him and softened at the uncertainty in his eyes. "No. Of course not. Mom can cook well enough—she's no Maria, mind you, but she won't poison you. I'm just not sure what she's going to want to talk about."

"I can think of a few things a grandmother-to-be might be curious about."

So could she. And that was part of the problem. Would her mother push and ask questions about marriage? Or plans for them to move in together? The latter was more likely— although maybe Mom's new Christianity would encourage her to see marriage as a viable institution, wouldn't it? Ugh. It was all so confusing. Indigo didn't have any answers. And she wasn't sure she wanted to hear whatever answers Joaquin had up his sleeve. "Just don't let her make you feel pressured, okay?"

"Not possible." He pressed his lips to her temple. "Have they done the sheep yet?"

"No. They're next."

Joaquin nodded. "Want me to grab the alpaca fleeces and haul them over to the fiber cabin for you?"

She blew out a breath. "I still haven't decided where I'm going to wash them. I don't want to clog up the pipes in the cabin, so I don't think I'll use the tub, which was my original thought. But it's still cold enough, I'm not sure I want to do it outside, either."

"It's not too cold to be shearing, is it?"

"Nah. They'll be fine. And they have shelters if we get a cold snap." She drummed her fingers on the top rail of the fence. "Yeah, I guess go ahead and take them over for me. Thanks."

"We've got some galvanized tanks hanging around in one of the storage rooms in the stable. Would those work for washing?"

"Why do you have those?"

He chuckled. "The setup we have in the stable today was a lot of years in the making. Morgan babies the horses. They didn't always live in the Ritz. Point is, we have big tubs."

"Those are perfect. Too bad there's not space in the stable to do the work." That would keep her out of the elements, too.

"Might be. I feel like there's some empty space—or at least an area that could be cleared for a temporary project. Want me to ask?"

"Would you?"

He nodded. "Course. I'll go do that now. If there is a place, I'll probably stay and help get it set up."

"You know what I need?"

Joaquin pulled his cell out of his pocket. "If I can't figure it out, I can look it up or text you."

Indigo laughed. "All right. I'll be by when the sheep are finished. And seriously, don't sweat dinner tonight."

"Easy for you to say." He winked and headed off in the direction of the stable.

Indigo turned, starting slightly.

Greg was standing close, hands in his pockets. "I like him better than the other guy."

Had nobody liked Wingfeather? Indigo frowned. Why hadn't anyone said something? Or, maybe they had and she just hadn't heard it. "Me, too."

Greg laughed. "Glad to hear it. We're ready to do the sheep. Anything we need to know?"

"I've got one who's expecting, I'll point her out. Otherwise, no. Same flock as last year." Minus a few she'd sold to other fiber farms. But that didn't matter to Greg. He charged by the animal and she'd given him an accurate count when she'd made the booking.

Greg fell into step beside her as they switched pens. "You've got a good operation here. I saw you're selling yarn online now, too?"

"And in person. Although I think in the two months I've been open we've had three or four customers, total." Indigo shrugged.

"Yeah? You have a shop?"

She nodded.

"Think when we're finished here I could take a peek? Sarah's gotten into knitting—getting better with each piece she makes. I think she'd go crazy over yarn that wasn't a cotton-poly blend from the craft store."

Indigo winced. "She'd better. That stuff is gross."

He laughed. "Cheaper though. Good for learning."

"I guess." She exaggerated a shudder. "My mom's over there now—I've started her on the carding drum and she's picked it up fast."

"You're processing for folks, too?"

"Yeah. A little of this, a little of that, and suddenly there's a living. You know how it is."

"I do." Greg grinned and pointed to where the pregnant ewe was huddled in the corner of pen. "She's expecting?"

Indigo looked over where he was pointing and nodded. "She's been hiding a lot lately."

"Hm. We'll do her first. You might want to keep an eye on her. Make sure you're ready when she drops those lambs."

"You think multiples?"

Greg shrugged. "Finnsheep tend that way. Never bet against genetics."

He was right. She didn't need more lambs right now. They had the space to expand the pens, if they needed, but the amount of wool she was getting was at the top end of what she could profitably process. There was a point where she'd have to decide if she needed to stop taking fleeces from others and bet it all on her own stock. She wasn't there yet, but every new baby moved her a little closer.

Unless she wanted to sell some of them. But that was its own headache. She wasn't knowingly going to sell them for meat, no matter how tasty people said they were. She shuddered.

"You okay?"

"Yeah. Just thinking."

"I'll leave you to it." Greg nodded, then let out a sharp whistle and his helper came jogging over. "Let's get this done. You're sure you've got time for us to see the shop before we go?"

"Absolutely. Least I can do." Indigo pushed her worries about the herd to the back of her mind and watched as Greg maneuvered her expecting ewe into what was basically a sitting type position. It was comfortable for the sheep—even though it didn't look that way at first glance—and it kept them from kicking and wiggling, which kept them safer during the shearing process.

Maybe while they worked their way through the sheep, she'd go check on Joaquin in the stables. Her heart leapt at the thought. Seeing him now was an elemental pleasure that she felt to the soles of her feet.

He'd said he loved her at lunch a few days ago—was it really only three days? He hadn't pushed her for a response.

Did she love Joaquin?

How was she even supposed to know?

She was attracted to him, absolutely. She knew, without a shadow of a doubt, that he was going to be a good father to his little girl. He'd also be there for Indigo through thick and thin. Joaquin was just the kind of guy who stuck.

Even if it wasn't the best decision for him. He'd do the right thing, no matter the personal cost.

Which meant Indigo needed to think clearly.

Her steps slowed as she approached the stable. Did he really love her, or was he still caught up in the idea that he was going to do right by her and the baby?

Everybody left at some point. Was she fooling herself to believe Joaquin would be any different?

"DATE NUMBER FIFTEEN."

"What was that, hon?" Betsy smiled as she glanced over at Indigo.

Her cheeks heated. She hadn't meant to say that aloud. "Nothing. Just counting up."

"The baby?"

She could lie. It might get her grandmother to drop the subject. But the easy and convenient lie wasn't something she was supposed to be excited about anymore. Honestly, sometimes she wished living for Jesus was as easy as accepting Him as her savior had been. "No. Dates with Joaquin. Tonight is number fifteen."

Betsy patted her hand over her heart. "That's sweet. And a little romantic."

"Not really." Indigo winced. "I mean, yeah, now. But I only agreed to go on forty dates with him because I felt backed into a corner."

Maria brought a mug of tea over and leaned on the counter,

smirking. "Joaquin always struck me as someone who'd be persistent when it mattered."

"Yeah, well, that seems to be the case." Indigo shifted uneasily on her stool. It didn't seem right to have this conversation with her sister-in-law and grandmother. "He's a good guy."

"Yes, he is." Betsy held Indigo's gaze. "I'm glad you see that."

Indigo fought the urge to hunch her shoulders. She hadn't done anything wrong. Better to try and shift the conversation away from her relationship. She looked at Maria. "Have any big anniversary plans? One year is coming up fast."

"Three weeks." Maria beamed and lifted her mug to take a sip.

"Maybe Wayne and I could keep Calvin and the two of you could get away for the weekend. You could head into Santa Fe, or down to Albuquerque and do something, just the two of you. With the baby coming in June, you should take advantage of it when you can."

Betsy made it sound like parents never got a minute to themselves. That hadn't been the case when she was growing up. Her parents often left Azure in charge and took off for a day—sometimes overnight. How old had Azure been? Eight? Nine? Probably too young, now that Indigo thought it through.

Did Joaquin realize what he was volunteering for? Would he get knee deep in it and decide it was too much?

Her stomach twisted.

Betsy and Maria chatted more, tossing ideas back and forth, while Indigo watched her future flash before her eyes.

She wasn't someone who needed to go out every night. Not even every week. But she did like the occasional break. Was that really something parents couldn't do?

"What do you think, Indigo?" Maria smiled over the edge of her mug.

Indigo tried to figure out what they might have asked her. "I'm sorry. I missed it. Woolgathering."

Maria laughed. "Professional hazard, I imagine."

Indigo smiled. "Something like that."

"Betsy was wondering if your mom might want to have Calvin one night. If Cyan and I took off for the weekend, they could keep him one night, and Elise could take the other?"

Indigo shrugged. "Sure. I don't see why not. Or," she glanced at Betsy, "what if Mom came here for the weekend and the four of you could hang together? I know she'd probably like that better."

"You don't think she'd want alone time?" Betsy folded her hands on the counter. "Wayne and I have had so much extra time with Calvin, we certainly don't mind sharing."

"You should ask her. I imagine she'd be happier with more people, but I could be wrong. Either way, I know she'd be happy to help. You and Cyan should definitely make some plans."

Maria grinned and rubbed a hand over her pregnant belly. "Okay. If you're sure, we'll do that. Maybe I'll set it up and surprise Cyan."

Indigo chuckled. "I bet he'd love that. My brother doesn't strike me as someone who plans romantic getaways."

"You might be surprised." Maria waggled her eyebrows.

"Oh, yuck." Indigo rolled her eyes. "You can keep that to yourself."

Betsy chuckled and slipped off the stool. "I think I'll walk down to the fiber cabin and talk to Elise. You heading that way, Indigo?"

"No. I should go check on the fleeces I have soaking. It's probably time to wring them out and see if they're clean enough or if they need another round of washing. But I can walk as far as the stable with you."

"That sounds good." Betsy pinned Maria with her gaze.

"Don't you over do anything. You've got two solid months before that baby is due, and I don't want you pushing yourself."

"All right, Betsy. I'll be sure to take a break when I need one. I'm going to put some chicken in the fridge to marinate for lunch tomorrow, if that works for you."

"Whatever you want. Ready, Indigo?"

"Yeah. Thanks for lunch, Maria." Indigo got down from the stool and pushed it back under the lip of the counter that they sat at to eat lunch.

"So, fifteen dates, was it?" Betsy held open the mudroom door and waited for Indigo to go through.

Indigo didn't bother to sigh. Apparently she hadn't managed to change the topic—or at least not permanently. "That's right."

"Everything's going well? Am I going to get to plan another wedding soon?"

She didn't know what to say. No answer seemed like it would be the right one. Joaquin certainly hoped that was the case. Indigo was still firmly on the "nope" side of the fence. But she also didn't want to disappoint her grandmother. Or Joaquin.

"I guess we'll see."

16

Easter Sunday at Hope Ranch was always thought provoking. Joaquin tucked his hands into the pockets of his slacks and looked at the large cross that was now covered in flowers. It was a new-ish tradition at the ranch, but it was one that he hoped they'd keep around for a long time to come. The transformation of the stark wood to colorful array of life was a picture he wouldn't be able to make as easily with words.

He needed the reminder in his own life.

He was a new creation in Christ.

Joaquin sighed and turned toward the main house. He didn't want to be late for Maria's big meal, either.

"You okay?" Indigo was waiting near the stables. She held out her hand.

"I'm good. How are you feeling?" He took her hand and they walked slowly toward the Hewitts' house.

"No complaints. I mean, I can drum some up if you need them. The pregnancy books aren't kidding when they talk about the weird aches that come from growing a baby. Those aside, though, I'm good." She smiled and bumped his hip with hers. "I was thinking how different it is to experience Easter now that I know Jesus."

Joaquin chuckled. "I imagine."

"Mom and Dad—and now, looking back, it was probably all Dad—were big on the bunny. They'd leave little rabbit footprints in the grass and piles of jelly beans from where he'd poo when he was hiding eggs. We sang the Peter Cottontail song. I think I was in high school before I realized there was anything else that Easter might be about." She sighed. "I don't understand, still, why Dad was so mean about the grandparents."

"I think, sometimes, when you're kicking back against the people who love you because you're trying to make your own way, it's easy to take it too far. I see it in myself sometimes, when I want to do something that I know is wrong, something I know is going to make Jesus unhappy but I just want it, I'll vilify anyone and everyone who has the temerity to suggest I think or pray about it." It was one of the reasons he'd eased away from everyone but Indigo at Skye's wedding reception. That instant attraction between them had always been leading one direction. He'd fought it off during the wedding and right after, but then at the reception, when everyone else was paired up and in their happy twosomes, it all crashed in on him.

He reached for the door and held it for Indigo, praying again for Jesus to help him forgive himself.

"I guess. Is it wrong that I'm mad that he took them away from me?" Indigo's gaze met his.

That was tricky ground. "It's not wrong to be hurt and to wish things had been different. But being mad at him isn't going to do anything but eat you up inside. Forgiveness is hard. But always worth it."

Indigo nodded slowly.

Joaquin chalked up her lack of response beyond that to the fact that they'd made it to the dining room. Skye, Maria, and

Cyan were still shuttling dishes from the kitchen to the table. Everyone else had taken their seats.

Elise grinned and patted the back of the chair beside her. "I saved the two of you space over here."

"Thanks." Joaquin followed Indigo around the table and held out the chair beside her mom for her before taking his own.

Elise reached across Indigo and patted his arm.

Skye set a bowl down then took the seat beside Morgan. Maria and Cyan claimed the last two empty seats with Calvin between them.

Wayne cleared his throat. "Now that we're all here, let's pray."

Joaquin closed his eyes and tried to focus on Wayne's words. There were so many distractions. The chairs were close together to accommodate all twelve of them, so Indigo's leg brushed against his. Other chairs squeaked. Clothes rustled. But Indigo filled his senses.

He loved her. He'd told her that a couple of times. She always smiled and blushed prettily, but she never said the words back.

Would she?

Was he enough for her? Sure, he was the father of the little girl she carried, but what else did he have to offer her? He was just a ranch hand. Anyone could take care of her animals—it wasn't hard. There were literally hundreds of websites that could tell you how to do it. He knew, because that was how he'd learned it in the first place. He was never going to be some kind of exotic artisan like Wingfeather.

And okay, sure, she didn't bring the guy up—ever—but his shadow still loomed over Joaquin. She'd been with Wingfeather a lot of years before she came here. What if she wasn't saying "I love you" because she was still in love with the other guy and waiting—hoping—for him to come back?

Indigo's elbow connected lightly with his ribs.

Joaquin looked up, heat burning across his cheeks.

"Pass the peas?" Indigo pointed to the bowl.

"You can have mine." Joaquin made a mock shudder.

"I saw that." Maria pointed her fork at him from across the table. "Try to be a better example to Calvin, would you?"

"I didn't stick out my tongue." It was the best he was going to be able to do. Peas were evil. He was relatively sure peas had been on that tree in the garden and that was why God warned Adam and Eve off.

Calvin laughed. "I like peas, Mom. It's those white carrots I don't like."

"Parsnips." Maria frowned. "Try one, okay?"

"I guess."

Joaquin took the platter of carrots and—who knew—parsnips. He'd thought they were white carrots, too. Glancing over at Calvin, he shot the boy a wink and scooped a few of each onto his plate.

"While everyone is greedily heaping food onto their plates in celebration of the Resurrection . . ." Royal scooted his chair back as every head at the table swiveled in his direction. He stood and took Sophie's hand. " . . . I've been trying to think of creative ways to do this for a month now, and last night I realized that as much as I might enjoy something crazy, Sophie wouldn't. And, in fact, maybe even this is going to be too much, but I'm so grateful to my family, I wanted you to be part of it."

Sophie's mouth dropped open, and she slapped her free hand over it.

Royal dropped to his knee, still holding her other hand. "Sophie, will you do me the honor of becoming my wife?"

"Of course I will!" Sophie launched herself off her chair into Royal's arms.

Joaquin laughed and joined in with the applause of everyone around the table as she knocked him back onto his rear.

"All right you two, save it for when you're alone." Cyan flicked a green bean at them, grinning when it smacked Royal in the ear and the two broke apart.

"Sorry." Royal rubbed his ear where the vegetable had hit him and climbed to his feet before offering Sophie a hand up.

"Where's my ring?" Sophie held out her hand.

Indigo laughed. "You tell him, Soph."

Royal reached up and rubbed the back of his neck. "I thought maybe we could go down to Santa Fe and pick something out on your next day off."

"Hm. That's only working because I love you." Sophie pressed her lips to Royal's.

"I love you, too."

"Awww." Betsy patted her heart, her eyes twinkling. "I imagine the two you need to go see Sophie's folks when you're finished eating."

Royal nodded. "That was the agreement."

Sophie rolled her eyes as she resumed her seat. "Of course, it was."

Conversations picked back up around the table now that the show was over. Joaquin sat back, mechanically bringing his fork to his mouth and working his way through the food on his plate. He couldn't have said what the flavors were.

He was happy for Royal and Sophie. They were a good match and seemed to have settled into a rhythm that would last well into their first years as a married couple. His gaze darted to Indigo. Didn't she want that? Especially with a baby on the way?

Elise caught his eye and the smile she sent him seemed almost apologetic. Could she see where his thoughts were trending? He worked to school his expression and tune back into the talk happening near him. There was time. The baby wasn't due for four months.

"Why can't I stay with Uncle Royal?" Calvin's voice rose above the rest of the conversation.

"Because your grandparents are excited to have some special time with you." Maria frowned and cast a worried glance over at Elise.

"You two going somewhere?" Joaquin tried to work out what the problem was. The boy's grandparents and uncle all lived in the same place. Surely they'd share the responsibility of taking care of him.

"It's our one-year anniversary at the end of the month. I found a cute bed-and-breakfast in Albuquerque and figured Cyan and I could take a weekend. It was pointed out that this is probably the last time we'll have that luxury before the baby comes." Maria's hand rubbed circles on her belly.

Joaquin nodded. She was due sooner than Indigo—June, maybe? The doctor had said something about not traveling far toward the end of things. He opened his mouth to offer a suggestion, but Elise started speaking first.

"Maybe we can split the time. You could spend one night with me and your other grandparents here at the big house and the second night in Royal's cabin, with him?" She glanced over at Royal, her eyebrows lifted.

"Sure. I'd like that. Sounds like the best of both worlds, bud. If it's okay with your mom and dad, of course." Royal tossed the conversational ball deftly back to Maria and Cyan.

Maria sighed. "You're sure you don't mind, Elise?"

"I'm sure." She smiled gently at Calvin. "We're still getting to know each other, right, Calvin?"

He nodded.

"Oh, Mom. Calvin." Cyan's frustrated expression as he

looked between the two of them would have been amusing if it hadn't been obvious that he was more upset with his step-son than anyone. "Thanks, Mom."

"It's really fine." Elise reached for the platter of ham.

Was she protesting just a little too much? Joaquin looked at Indigo. She'd started patting her mother's leg gently. Indigo, at least, seemed to realize Calvin's unwitting rejection had hurt. Kids spoke their minds. Was he ready to take that on?

There were a few years before it was a real concern, but the enormity of Indigo's pregnancy crashed over him.

She was having a baby, yes. But that child would grow up and need him. Need both of them. For a lot of years yet to come.

He wiped his damp palms on his napkin and reached for his water with a shaking hand.

He could do this. He would do this.

As long as he could convince Indigo to let him.

17

Indigo watched the new lambs in the paddock. The birth had gone well the day after Easter, and the twin lambs were healthy and playful. Now, a little over a week old, they seemed to have settled into the routine of sheep life.

Joaquin took good care of them. And the alpacas. Indigo had eased up on how often she came to the pens to check on things. Really, she only stopped by when she wanted to see the animals for the sake of seeing them. There wasn't anything she needed to do for them that wasn't already being done.

It was a good feeling.

"Hey."

Indigo turned at Joaquin's voice and smiled. Her mouth watered. He was a picture, no question. "Hey, yourself."

"I looked for you at the stables. I guess you finished washing and drying all the fleeces?"

"I did. Morgan said he'd get everything put away in that room but that I was welcome to use it whenever I needed."

Joaquin chuckled. "He told me the same thing. I did get a chance to help him with that though, when I went looking for you."

"Thanks." She reached out and took his hand. "The lambs are doing well."

"They are." He stepped closer and slid an arm around her waist. The warmth of his body by hers made her swallow. Shouldn't that jolt be wearing off by now? "What are you up to today?"

"I've been trying to decide if I want to dye the fleece before I card and spin it, or if I should stick to my usual process."

"Is there a reason to change it up?"

Indigo shrugged. She probably shouldn't give words to the general restlessness inside her. She'd stayed at the commune for years—so it wasn't as if she didn't know how to stick—but in Arizona, she'd been alone more often than not. In some ways, maybe even a lot of them, she missed that. At Hope Ranch, there was always someone around. She lived with Mom. Mom was at the fiber cabin most of the time, too. If Indigo broke away to visit the animals, she ran into Joaquin—or any number of other people who were also moving around and going about their daily work. And that wasn't bad. It was different.

Everything was different.

Maybe she'd jumped into too much change all at once.

"I'm sure you'll figure it out." He shifted so they faced each other and tugged her close. His hands slid to her hips and locked her in place as his lips descended to hers.

For one flash of an instant, Indigo braced to run. When their mouths met, she melted into him. Her hands slid up his chest to his shoulders. Her fingers curled into his shirt, clinging to him as the kiss stole her breath and left her knees weak.

Time stood still. There was only Joaquin.

He shifted and kissed her jaw at the base of her ear then trailed kisses down her neck.

Indigo's head dropped back, and she drew in a quick breath.

"Well. This is interesting."

Indigo tore her gaze away from the desire in Joaquin's eyes and frowned at the woman striding toward them. She bore enough family resemblance that there was only one person she could be. "Jade."

"That's me." The woman's grin was sharp and smug. "You're Indigo, I assume? The old woman at the main house said I might find you here, and that you'd be a good choice to take me to some camp to find Skye."

"Is she expecting you?" The "old woman" had to be Betsy. Did Jade know who Betsy was? What she was to Jade? Why was she even here?

"Where would be the fun in that?"

"I can take her over to the camp, if you want." Joaquin's voice was quiet, as though he was working hard to keep himself in check. Apparently Indigo wasn't the only one bristling at Jade.

"It's okay." Indigo rubbed Joaquin's arm, hoping to soothe him. "I don't mind. I'll see you later."

Joaquin searched her face before nodding once, giving her a quick squeeze, and heading off toward the stable while he worked his phone out of his back pocket.

Indigo studied her half-sister and tried to find a smile to offer. She jerked her head toward the path that would lead them to the camp. "This way."

"Wait. Don't you have a car or something?"

Indigo glanced over her shoulder and watched Jade hurry to catch up. She wasn't wearing shoes suited for walking around a ranch. The peep-toe booties were probably fashionable, and they definitely went along with her outfit, but they were better suited for a city somewhere. "Sure. But it's not far."

Jade groaned. "Seriously. You're not going to drive me?"

"Nope. You probably had a long drive to get here. A walk is just what you need." Besides, it wasn't far. Maybe a quarter of a mile. Indigo pulled her cell from her pocket and shot Skye a quick text to let her know what was heading her way. No reason her younger sister should be blindsided the same way she had been.

Of course, with the way Joaquin had been kissing her, any interruption would have blindsided her simply because she'd forgotten that the rest of the world existed.

"So who's the cowboy?"

"He's not a cowboy." The denial was immediate, just like it would have been if Joaquin had been there. "He's a ranch hand. His name's Joaquin."

"Good looking."

Indigo scowled at Jade. "Yes. And spoken for."

Jade held up her hands. "I still have eyes. There any more like him hanging around up here?"

Tommy was the only single guy left and Indigo wasn't going to throw him to the wolves. Indigo ignored the question and pointed to the lodge, which was just visible in the distance. "That's where we're headed. Skye and Morgan live there. Skye runs the camp and Morgan runs the stable at the ranch. She might not have too much time for us. She mentioned there's a weekend retreat coming in on Friday. She's working today to get everything set up."

"Big job."

Indigo bristled. "Skye's quite competent. And she has help when she needs it."

"I'm just saying. Are you always this prickly?"

Indigo stopped and whirled, hands on her hips. "Why are you here?"

"I have as much right to be here as you do." Jade jutted out her chin.

Indigo frowned. Jade was right, but that didn't mean the retort went down well. "Haven't you caused enough drama in our family?"

"I just want what I'm owed."

"Nobody owes you anything."

"That's a matter of opinion." Jade stepped closer so her toes bumped Indigo's. "And I'm not inclined to care about anyone's opinion but my own."

Indigo took a deep breath and stiffened to keep from shaking. Heat flashed through her veins. She pointed toward the lodge. "That's where you're headed. I don't think you should have any trouble getting there from here."

"Wait. You're not taking me all the way there?"

Indigo shook her head.

"Seriously?"

"Why would I, Jade? You don't want to be part of this family. You didn't come here looking to connect and be friends—or even open the door to friendship down the road. All you've done is create drama. I heard about your dinner with Royal. I saw firsthand exactly what you think of us when I got my copy of the letter from your attorney."

Jade's cheeks turned red, and she looked away.

Indigo barreled on. "So, no. I don't want to walk you all the way to the lodge and politely introduce you to my sister, because I don't think you're here to meet her in person. Or to meet me in person. Or to get to know anyone here on the ranch at all. You're only here because you want something, and I for one intend to make it my life's mission to see that you don't get it."

Jade's jaw dropped. Her eyes flashed. "How dare you."

"How dare I?" Indigo stomped her foot. "My dad didn't do the right thing by you—no question—but from what I understand about your mother, she wasn't going to take what he was able to give anyway. And now you're here to stir up more drama? After we gave you an equal share of everything that my dad should have left to my mom to take care of her?"

"He didn't take care of my mom, either."

"No. He didn't. And that's on him, not us. But when your mom passed, she left you something, which means she was doing okay for herself. What Dad left my mom isn't enough to keep her until she dies. So she's here, miserable, living on the handouts of people who are strangers to her. And you made it more necessary than it would have been."

Jade frowned. "What do you mean?"

"Please. Don't act like you don't know all this. I know Skye texts you."

"I don't, though. Skye never said anything." Jade drew an X over her heart. "I swear."

Indigo huffed out a breath, and the anger faded. She'd never been good at holding on to her anger. She scowled at Jade and jerked her head toward the lodge before stomping down the path toward it. She didn't bother to see if her half-sister was following before she started speaking. "Mom and Dad weren't married, which means the kids got everything. There was nothing for Mom, since he didn't have a will. Didn't matter much, there wasn't a lot to have anyway, but we split it six ways, gave you your portion, and then we all gave the rest back to Mom so she'd have something. But you can do the math. Multiply what you got by five and tell me how long that'd keep you in potatoes and peas."

Jade's breath was coming fast as she stretched her legs to keep up with Indigo's strides. "I thought they'd bought a house."

Indigo snorted. "Oh yeah. Dad bought a house. One with a mortgage they couldn't afford and an enormous balloon payment that came due the month before he died."

"Oh."

Yeah. *Oh.*

Indigo slowed her steps a tiny bit. That financial obligation probably hadn't helped his health any. Maybe his death wasn't completely Jade's fault. Not that she was innocent, but ... darn it. Indigo was going to have to forgive the woman, wasn't she?

"This is the lodge. Skye said she'd be—" Indigo broke off when Skye stepped out onto the porch with a hesitant smile and a wave.

Jade lagged behind.

"Come on. This is why you're here, right?" Indigo glanced at Jade and sighed. "Maybe if you give it a chance, without the big chip on your shoulder, you'll find this is a place you can belong."

Jade looked up, startled, and met Indigo's eyes. "But what about all that you just spewed at me?"

Indigo shrugged. "My grandparents—*our* grandparents—are big believers in Jesus."

Jade snorted.

"Yeah, well, I used to agree with you. Then I came here. Now?" Indigo shrugged. "I've had a change of heart. And I know that they—my grandparents and Jesus both—would want me to forgive you. So I do. Or will. It'll probably take me a little bit. But I'll keep trying till it sticks."

Skye ran down the porch steps and threw her arms around Indigo. "Oh. I caught the last bit—your voice carries. But that's exactly it, exactly the point."

Indigo chuckled and hugged Skye quickly before taking a step back. "Skye, Jade. Jade, Skye. I imagine you two have a lot to talk about, and I have wool to process."

"Um. Thanks."

Indigo frowned at Jade. "For what?"

"For bringing me over to Skye. And the conversation."

Skye shot Indigo a look that all but promised Indigo would be explaining all of that later.

For now, Indigo managed a tight smile and a nod. "See you later."

Skye was already dragging Jade by the hand into the lodge,

chattering at her, when Indigo turned and started walking back toward the main part of the ranch.

She was going to forgive Jade.

What had she been thinking? Oh, sure, she was pretty sure that was what Jesus would want her to do. And it was probably also what Joaquin and her grandparents would want her to do.

But just about anything else seemed like it would be easier.

18

"I'm so sorry."

Joaquin smiled and reached for Indigo's hand. "You said that already."

"I know. But it doesn't change the fact that I feel awful. We don't have to count this as one of the forty dates, if you don't want to."

Joaquin struggled to keep a frown from forming. Was she still counting? Weren't they past that? Was she only with him because she'd given her word? "It's fine. We're going to have a meal and play some board games. I'd say that counts as having the necessary date elements."

"With my mom. And my grandparents. And my nephew. And, oh yes, my half-sister." Indigo glanced around the cabin before shrugging and starting toward the door. "I'm not excited about it. I can't fathom why you would be."

"I get to spend time with you. That's enough." He squeezed her fingers and pulled open the door. Even though they were nearing the end of April, there was a bite in the air when the sun was setting. He nudged her with his elbow and pointed toward the mountains. "Look."

Indigo looked over and gasped.

"Never gets old, does it?" Joaquin studied the purplish red that the setting sun painted the mountainsides. It was why the mountain range had gotten the name *Sangre de Cristo*—the blood of Christ—though it had never really looked like blood to him. It was still a sight worth stopping and drinking in.

"It doesn't. Although I don't remember to look as often as I should."

"I don't think any of us do." Joaquin tugged her hand and started walking toward the main house. "All the more reason to pause for a minute when we have the chance."

"I sure hope Maria didn't make supper for us before she and Cyan left for their weekend."

"Knowing Maria, she not only made us supper, she also stocked Betsy and Wayne's fridge for more meals than they'd manage in a week."

Indigo snickered. "True. She really loves it though, doesn't she?"

"Seems to. I guess you never know what's going to catch someone's eye. It's not like I grew up with plans to be a generic ranch hand in New Mexico." He shook his head. It was still a point of contention between him and his parents. They had, mostly, accepted it at this point, but it definitely factored into the frequency with which he contacted them. "Do you think you'd like to go to visit my folks sometime after the baby's born?"

Indigo's eyebrows lifted. "Um."

"You don't have to answer now. Just think about it. They're excited about the baby. And about you."

"Why would they be excited about me?"

"Because I love you. Isn't that reason enough?"

Silence again. Because of course she wasn't going to say the words back to him. He was trying not to push—he really was—but it got harder every time.

Finally, she nodded. "Of course, it is. I'm not sure how old babies have to be before they can travel."

"That's a point." He reached for the handle of the back door. "I guess I'll see if they can come out here. They've never been to the ranch—they might like that just as much. Maybe more."

Indigo's smile didn't reach her eyes. "Great."

"There you are!" Calvin barreled into Joaquin's legs. "Grandma Betsy said we had to wait for you and Aunt Indigo to get here before we could eat, and I'm *starving*."

Joaquin laughed and ruffled the boy's hair. "Sorry, champ, didn't mean to keep you waiting. What are we having?"

"Tamales. Mom said it was only fair that we had something special since she and Dad would be, too."

"Yum. Your mom makes the best tamales in the world. If I'd known that was on the menu, I would've hurried Indigo along."

Calvin laughed and dashed through the kitchen hollering that it was finally time to eat.

"Tamales are a lot of work." Indigo sniffed the kitchen air. "They smell good."

Betsy came into the kitchen, laughing at something Calvin said as he danced and jumped next to her. "They do smell good, don't they? I told her not to bother, but she was adamant. I invited Tommy, too, since she made so many. That's all right, isn't it?"

"Of course, it is. How can we help?" Joaquin walked to the sink to wash his hands. There was strain showing around Betsy's eyes if someone knew where to look. He'd been around the ranch long enough that he did. It was probably Jade. He hadn't had much exposure to her, but what he'd had was plenty. Even though Indigo said she was going to forgive the woman—and good on her for that, no question—Jade couldn't leave Hope Ranch soon enough for Joaquin's taste.

"Would you mind getting them out of the oven? She put

them in there to stay warm. And she made a handful of them vegan—they're marked with toothpicks." Betsy sent Indigo a tired smile. "Then maybe you could put them on platters? Indigo, hon, would you mind helping me set the table?"

"Of course not." Indigo washed her hands before pulling plates down out of the cabinet. She pointed at Calvin. "How about you get the silverware?"

"Okay!" Calvin yanked out a drawer and started grabbing forks.

Betsy leaned against the counter and sighed. "I'll get the salad out of the fridge, then. The tamales are the bulk of the meal. I talked her out of rice and beans."

"That's good. This'll be fine. Betsy, you look beat." Joaquin slid one dish of tamales onto the island and turned for another. Indigo and Calvin headed out of the kitchen with the plates and flatware.

Betsy watched them leave before she craned her neck to look into the living room and shook her head. "Jade. I don't know what to do there, Joaquin. She's so angry. And sometimes she'll get it under control, and we'll have a good conversation, but she has so much hurt. I just don't know how to help her."

Joaquin took down the two big platters they used for Sunday lunch and started transferring tamales. "Seems to me all we can do is pray for her. From what Skye has said, and Royal to some degree, Jade doesn't know Jesus. That's a place to start."

"You're right." Betsy patted Joaquin's hand before picking up the first platter. "It just feels like there should be more than that."

He understood that feeling. And it wasn't as if following Jesus had suddenly fixed everything between him and Indigo. In fact, sometimes it seemed like it was worse. He shouldn't even think that. It was good that Indigo was growing in her relationship with Jesus. That was the most important thing. But it often seemed like she was working on that relationship and completely ignoring the one with him. Where did he factor into her long-term plans?

Maybe the better question was *did* he factor into those plans at all?

Joaquin sighed and moved to the fridge to get the salad. Maria had covered the bowl and serving tongs with plastic wrap. He set it on the counter and pulled off the plastic. Was it already dressed? She usually put something on the top. He reached in and snagged a grape tomato and popped it in his mouth. Nodding, he stuck the tongs into the greenery. Dressed and ready to go. He shifted the salad bowl to the crook of his elbow and picked up the platter of tamales with his other hand before heading into the dining room.

"Oh, let me get that, dear." Betsy hurried around and took the platter. "I'm sorry. I was going to come back and help."

"It's fine. And now it's all here." He surveyed the table. Calvin was already seated and working on sliding a tamale onto his plate. Jade sat, arms crossed, at a seat separate from everyone. Tommy and Indigo were hovering at one end of the table looking unsure. Wayne and Elise were already sitting beside Calvin. He glanced over at Betsy. "Do you care where we sit?"

Betsy pulled out the chair beside Wayne and sat. "Anywhere is fine."

Joaquin blew out a breath and scooted a little closer to Jade. He motioned for Indigo and Tommy to join him. "Skye and Morgan couldn't make it?"

"No. There's a small group at the lodge and they needed to be there in case." Jade frowned, and then seemed to actively relax her face. "I appreciate you including me. It smells good."

"Mom makes the best tamales. Who are you? I'm Calvin. I'm nine. When Mom married Dad, it made Grandma Betsy and

Grandpa Wayne my *real* grandparents. And I got aunts and uncles and everything. It's pretty cool."

Jade smiled.

Everyone else at the table laughed.

"That's a pretty good deal, I have to admit." Tommy reached for a platter of tamales and poked at the toothpicks in some. "Why do some have sticks?"

"They're vegan." Indigo reached for one and slid it onto her plate. "Thanks."

"Doesn't the baby need meat?" Jade took the salad bowl when it was passed her way.

Indigo shook her head. "Not necessarily. Although I've been adding dairy. The doctor's keeping an eye on things. If I need more or different protein, we'll figure it out."

Joaquin rubbed Indigo's leg under the table.

Betsy and Elise exchanged a look before Betsy spoke. "To answer your question, Calvin, that's your aunt Jade."

"Another aunt? Cool." Calvin studied Jade before nodding. "Did you bring a present?"

Jade visibly fought a grin. "Not this time. Next time, I will. Are you too old for dinosaurs?"

Calvin appeared to consider it. "Probably not. As long as they're not the cartoon baby ones. T-rex is pretty cool."

Jade nodded. "I always thought so, too."

"That was Dad's favor—" Indigo broke off when Elise let out a startled cry and jumped up. Her chair clattered to the floor and she fled the room. Indigo winced. "Sorry."

"It's okay." Joaquin shifted in his seat. An uncomfortable, awkward silence hung in the room. He cleared his throat. "Maybe I should go check on her."

"No. Let me. It was my mistake." Indigo sighed and stood. She turned and looked at Jade. "Dad loved the T-rex, too. Until the day he died, it was his favorite. Maybe you get that from him."

Joaquin watched her slip from the room. His heart ached for the whole family. Indigo's dad had made a huge mess and then left it for everyone else to clean up. It was why Joaquin was going to be part of his child's life, no matter what.

"I'm sorry. I—I shouldn't have come." Jade hung her head.

"I'm glad you did." Betsy set her fork down and waited for Jade to look up. "We're glad to open our home to anyone. Joaquin and Tommy know firsthand that you don't have to be blood for us to consider you family. But when you are? It's just more special."

"Why would you be that way?" Jade picked up her fork and poked at the food on her plate. "People must walk all over you."

Wayne chuckled. "Maybe. Sometimes. But neither Betsy nor I would change a thing. God has blessed us richly. How could we ever do anything other than share that blessing with the people who need it?"

Calvin's fork clattered on his plate. "Can I be excused?"

Joaquin shook his head. The kid had inhaled the plateful of food he'd been given. At least someone was doing justice to Maria's cooking.

"May I." Betsy corrected Calvin. "And yes. Wash your hands before you touch anything."

"Are we still playing Chinese checkers later? And having ice cream sundaes? Even if Grandma Elise is gone?"

"Course we are." Wayne patted the boy's arm. "Go wash up and read or play on your tablet a bit. I haven't finished enjoying your mom's hard work yet."

"Okay. Bye." Calvin darted from the room.

Joaquin chuckled and cut into his tamale. He wasn't really hungry anymore, but it didn't seem right not to eat. Would Indigo come back after she talked to her mom? Would Elise come back? This was supposed to be the night with all three grandparents—Royal was taking Calvin tomorrow. Surely Elise wouldn't want to miss out on time with her first grandchild.

Should he go help?

Joaquin looked around the table. No one else seemed to know what to do either.

19

Indigo opened the cabin door and stepped back to let in Joaquin. "Thanks for coming over."

Joaquin opened his arms.

Letting out her breath, Indigo stepped into them and laid her head on his shoulder. It was nice to have someone to share the burden, even a little. "I don't understand."

"She hasn't been home?"

Indigo shook her head. "And Grandma said she wasn't in any of the rooms up at their house. I just assumed—I didn't even think when she didn't come home last night. The plan was always for her to stay and do stuff with Calvin."

"You tried her cell?"

Indigo wiggled free of his embrace and stalked into the kitchen. She picked a cell phone off the counter and held it up. "No point. It's here."

"Oh."

"Yeah. Oh." Indigo wrapped her arms around herself. "What do I do?"

Joaquin rubbed the back of his neck. "First thing, let's pray."

"That's what Betsy said."

He smiled and stepped closer, drawing her back into his arms. "That's because she's a smart lady."

"I just feel like I should be doing something more useful."

"Prayer is useful." He rubbed little circles on her back. "I'll start."

Indigo tried to listen as Joaquin prayed for her mom. What was God going to do? Did He do big signs in the sky? Or some kind of aha moment where they'd all suddenly realize where she'd gone? It wasn't as if this wasn't exactly what happened in her life. People left. It was what they did. Probably there was some lack in her that made it easier for everyone to do, but she'd never been able to pin that down. Wingfeather had been good at offering his opinion—all the reasons he'd leave. Of course, he'd come back. Until he hadn't.

She forced her thoughts away from Wingfeather. Why did she keep thinking about him, anyway? That relationship was over. For all she knew, he was dead. And she had Joaquin, who said he loved her. She loved him. Even if the words got stuck somewhere in her chest.

Better to hold on to them, anyway. If her own mother was going to walk away, what would make someone like Joaquin stay?

Joaquin pressed his lips to her forehead. "We'll keep praying. I'm not sure there's a point to driving around aimlessly looking for her, though."

Indigo's eyes filled. He was right. "But what if—"

"Don't start imagining the worst, okay? She has her ID?"

Indigo nodded.

"And probably something that would indicate she's staying here. She's been going to church in town with your grandparents, so it's possible—probable even—that if something bad were to happen, they'd know to come tell someone at the ranch."

She didn't like it. "But—"

Joaquin cut her off by kissing her.

After a moment, Indigo sank into it, letting the sensations sweep her away and clear her mind of the stress and worry. She tugged at his shirt, untucking a little so she could sneak her hand in against his warm side.

HE GROANED AND EASED BACK, resting his forehead on hers. "Let's go open up the fiber cabin."

Indigo blinked. The fiber cabin? "I wasn't planning on opening today."

"You've got Saturday hours on your website. The work will help." Joaquin took her hand and squeezed. "And I'll feel better knowing you're there, keeping busy. Tommy and I need to do some maintenance at the camp today. That group Skye booked got rowdy last night and broke a window."

"It can't wait?"

"Not unless we want to risk having to do more repair because of weather damage. There's still the possibility of snow. I know we're nearing the end of April, but stranger things have happened. It's better to keep things weather tight." Joaquin opened the door to her cabin. "I'll walk you over there first, though."

Indigo bit her lip. Finally, she snagged her cell and her mom's and put them in her pockets. "All right."

Despite Joaquin's talk of snow, it was a cool spring morning. Little flowers poked their brave heads out in the meadow. The sheep and alpacas were happily munching away.

"Do you think she's okay?"

"I do. I think it's Jade, honestly."

Indigo nodded. "Probably. The dinosaur thing at dinner last night. I wasn't thinking."

"Why would you worry about that? Your mom is trying, but you have to admit this is a hard place to be."

That was an understatement. "I want to believe there's a way for Mom and Jade to at least have peace between them. Jade already seems softer. Maybe the tongue lashing I gave her when she first showed up sank in."

"I must have missed that."

Heat seared her cheeks. "I thought I mentioned it. I basically reminded her she wasn't the only victim of my dad's carelessness."

"That doesn't sound too bad."

Not on the surface. She could look back at how she'd handled it, though, and realize she hadn't done a superior job. There was no changing the past. If some good came out of it, if she and Jade were able to forge some kind of relationship, maybe then she'd figure out a way to stop regretting it.

Indigo shrugged and slipped the fiber-cabin key from her pocket. "You'll let me know if you hear anything about Mom?"

"You'll be the first. And the same goes, okay? I'm worried, too. But I'm trusting she'll be all right." He leaned in and kissed her—not the quick peck she'd expected, but a longer kiss full of heat that left her sighing when he pulled away. "I'll see you."

"Yeah. Bye." Indigo watched him stride toward the path that would take him out to the camp. He sure could walk.

"It's a good view, isn't it?" Jade smirked as she strolled up the road from the main house. "And that kiss looked hot."

Indigo bit back the snappy reply that hovered at the tip of her tongue. She could be nice. "It was."

Jade laughed.

"What brings you up this way?" Indigo finished unlocking

the cabin and stepped in, flipping on the lights and looking around the main room like she did every morning when she arrived. It was still a thrill. This little retail space had been a dream—not one she was ever going to share, of course, but still a dream—since she first agreed to Wingfeather's fiber farm idea.

Jade whistled. "This is more than I expected. Betsy said you had a fiber business, but this is the real thing."

How was she supposed to take that? "Thanks?"

Jade winced. "Sorry. It was meant to be a compliment. I'm trying, okay? It's . . . a lot of years to undo."

Indigo reached over and touched her half-sister's arm. "Me, too."

Jade grinned. "So here's the thing."

Uh-oh. That was a somewhat ominous beginning. Indigo flipped the sign in the window to "open" and moved to turn on the small Bluetooth speaker and get some music started.

"Knitting is kind of all the rage right now."

Indigo nodded. It was definitely gaining in popularity. "I'm not sure I'd go that far, but it's seeing a resurgence, for sure."

"I don't know how. And I was wondering if you thought you could teach me."

"Teach you to knit." Indigo froze. In theory she could. Classes were on her list of "someday" services.

"Yeah. Too hard? Too much? I'll understand if you say no. I just thought it was maybe a way that you and I could spend some time together."

"You're staying? Here?" Indigo's thoughts scattered.

"I was thinking about it. Betsy and Wayne thought it was a good idea. But if it's not, I don't have to."

"Don't you work?"

"Not right now." Jade's cheeks reddened. "There was a problem and the customer was out for blood and I was the natural choice for sacrificial lamb. So, to keep the client happy, I had to go."

"That doesn't seem right. Was it your fault?"

Jade shrugged. "Depends on how you look at it. It's the way PR jobs go. There's always the possibility that what you do isn't going to fly, and someone has to pay for it."

"That's surprisingly accepting of you."

Jade snorted. "I'm actually not usually the raging . . . well . . . *person* that your family has known me as. I'm sorry."

"You know what? I think I believe you." Indigo dropped to the sofa and shook her head. "Mom ran off last night. After the dinosaur thing—I thought she was just going to get some air and she'd come back after we all left. But apparently she didn't."

"I'm sorry for that, too." Jade perched on the arm of the sofa. "Would it be better if I left?"

"No." Indigo shook her head. "No, I don't think it would. Mom's an adult. And she and Dad had this stupid arrangement to start out with, so it wasn't as if she shouldn't have considered the possibility. Even if he promised. You're part of the family. You deserve to be here every bit as much as she does."

"I don't want to hurt her, though. Or hurt her more. I guess I hurt her just by existing."

"That's not on you." Indigo reached over and patted Jade's knee. "Let's get you some needles and see if you can make a scarf."

Jade wrinkled her nose. "Do I really have to start with a scarf?"

"You do. But if you do a good job with the first couple inches of stockinette, we'll add some fun to the pattern for the rest of it. Deal?"

"You're the expert."

Indigo chuckled. "Yes, I am. So look over the yarn and find what you like. I need to dig in the boxes in the back to find the needles I ordered to sell as sidelines. I haven't unpacked them yet."

While Jade stood and wandered to the wall of yarn, Indigo hurried down the hallway to the bedroom she'd designated as storage. She had plans to make it a useful storeroom—shelves and organization—but for now it was boxes stacked on top of each other. At least she knew which one had the needles in it. Or she thought she did.

"Is that you, Indigo?" Mom poked her head out of the door to a different bedroom.

"Mom? You're here." Her breath whooshed out and she ran over to wrap her mom in her arms and squeeze. "You scared the life out of me. What were you thinking?"

"I wasn't. I guess. I just got so mad . . . I don't expect you to understand." Mom pulled back and crossed her arms.

"Well, you should. We're all angry at Dad, but that's not Jade's fault." Indigo reached into her pocket and pulled out her mom's phone. She slapped it into Mom's hand. "You could at least have taken this."

Mom looked away. "Sorry."

"You should be." Indigo glanced over her shoulder. The hall was still clear. She lowered her voice. "Speaking of Jade, she's here. I'm going to teach her to knit. If you don't want to stay, that's fine, but you need to be polite when you leave."

Something flashed in her mom's eyes. Then she deflated. She nodded once. "I wouldn't mind a knitting lesson myself."

A tiny flicker of hope bloomed in Indigo's chest. "Really?"

Mom nodded. "Let's give it a try."

Indigo smiled and ducked into the storage room. She sorted through until she found the right box and dug out two sets of circular knitting needles, then she sat on the floor and texted Joaquin and Betsy.

Mom wasn't gone after all. That was good. But she'd still run off to begin with. And giving it a try didn't mean committing to stay.

She sighed as she stood and dusted off her pants. If everyone's first instinct was to leave, she'd still need to watch out. A well-protected heart was less likely to break.

Joaquin knocked on the door to the cabin Indigo shared with her mom. Nerves danced in his belly and made him frown. There was no need for that. They were just heading to church, like they did every Sunday. He glanced at the bouquet of mixed wildflowers he clutched. Well, okay, not exactly like every Sunday. Mother's Day was kind of a big deal. Especially since this would be Indigo's first.

"Hi." Indigo stepped back. "Come on in. I'm running late."

"There's time." Joaquin closed the doorway and hovered in the entry. "Go finish getting ready."

"There's coffee, if you need some. Mom made a full pot. It's part of why I'm running late."

Joaquin's eyebrows lifted, but Indigo had hurried back to the private areas of the cabin so he couldn't ask for an explanation. He strode into the kitchen and started opening cabinets. He didn't want coffee, but he could probably find something that would work as a vase and at least get the flowers in some water.

After looking around, he settled on a plastic pitcher. Why wouldn't two women living together have at least one vase? They could probably get one from Betsy—but maybe Joaquin should get Indigo one as a gift instead. He'd think on it. For now, the pitcher would do, even if it wasn't beautiful.

"Are those for me?" Indigo slipped her arm around his waist as he stood at the sink, filling the pitcher with water.

"They are. Your first Mother's Day. Seemed appropriate."

Indigo's hand moved to cover her belly, and her eyes filled. "Mother's Day."

Joaquin smiled and drew her into his arms. He pressed his lips to her forehead.

Indigo tipped her head and their lips met.

His eyes drifted closed, and he sank into the kiss.

Indigo scooted back. "We should go."

Right. Church. He nodded and gave her a quick peck before stepping away and offering her his hand. "Ready?"

"Yeah. Thanks for the flowers, Joaquin. I appreciate them."

"You're welcome. I love you." He waited a beat. She smiled and squeezed his hand, but that was it. He'd never considered himself insecure before, but maybe he was going to need to rethink that. What was it going to take for her to say the words?

Did she even feel that way about him in the first place? Maybe that was what was holding her back.

He tried to put it away as they drove off the ranch and into town. He listened to her chatting about the good conversations she'd been having with Jade. Over the last couple of weeks, the two of them—well three, if he included Skye, who seemed to do what she could to be part of it—were becoming thick as thieves. It was a good thing. Even Elise seemed to be warming, slightly, to Jade's presence.

Betsy and Wayne were elated. He saw it in their faces—they had their family here at the ranch, and nothing suited them better than that.

He made a mental note to reach out to Tommy and schedule some more game nights. Sitting around hoping to spend time with Indigo only to discover she'd made plans with Jade and Skye was getting old.

They tiptoed into church and slid into the back row while everyone was singing. Indigo had been handed a hot pink paper bag with a giant white bow on the top of it when they entered. He saw her poking at the top, trying to peek in.

He bumped her with his elbow and winked.

Indigo rolled her eyes, but set the bag down on the ground and focused on the screen at the front of the room that had the words for the song.

She didn't sing. Had she ever? Joaquin tried to think back and couldn't pin down whether or not he'd heard her. Maybe she was self-conscious about her voice. He'd gone through an awkward phase in college when he hadn't wanted to sing because he wasn't sure if he'd be perfectly on pitch. Then he'd heard a few of the people in the choir goof up—rather horribly —and he'd realized it wasn't about sounding good to others.

Now he sang loudly, and didn't pay attention to the side-eye when it came.

And it always came.

The sermon was on Proverbs 31. He shook his head and followed along as the pastor talked about the importance of a Godly mother.

Joaquin glanced over at Indigo's baby bump. His little girl was in there, growing and getting ready to meet the world in just three months. He had an app on his phone that gave him a daily update about what was happening as she grew. Maybe it was weird for the dad to do that—but it wasn't as if he and Indigo lived together and could talk about it whenever the mood struck. When they were together, they often avoided the topic of the baby.

He frowned.

She did tend to change the subject whenever he brought up

names. He got a say in that. And the baby would be a Rivera. Wouldn't she?

He scribbled a note. They needed to sit down and talk—not today; today was for celebrating moms—but soon. And he wasn't going to let her change the subject or distract him with those kissable lips.

When the service was over, they worked their way out to the truck. Seemed as though everyone noticed a pregnant woman on Mother's Day. And half of them wanted to know when they'd gotten married. At least they'd had the grace to leave it at "Oh" when either he or Indigo explained. Gosh, he wanted to fix that, too. But if she couldn't say she loved him back, there was no way she was going to be able to say "I do."

So he'd wait.

"I liked that sermon." Indigo reached for her seatbelt and stretched it around to click it in place, before sliding it under her baby belly. "I can weave and spin. And dye. Maybe I have something going for me, after all."

"You're amazing. I'm sorry you don't realize it."

She reached over and touched his leg. "Thank you. I saw you taking notes, too."

"Well, there were more things I wanted to remember later. Not really about the sermon." He cleared his throat and turned onto the road that would take them back to the ranch. "Like her name."

"Oh." She sighed. "I guess I need to figure that out."

Joaquin nodded. He didn't want to say more—regardless of the words that crowded their way forward—because it was obvious they'd have an argument if he did. There was probably some unwritten relationship rule about picking a fight on Mother's Day.

"Do you have names you wanted to suggest?"

He glanced over and one corner of his mouth lifted. "A

couple. I might have downloaded a baby name book onto my e-reader."

She laughed. "You didn't."

He shrugged.

"You did?"

"Seemed like we ought to have one to look through. We could spend some time together going through it, if you wanted."

She frowned. "I guess I'm surprised you want a say."

"In my baby girl's name? Why wouldn't I want a say?"

"Well, it's not like we're married. I mean, yeah, sure technically she's your baby girl, but it's not like she's yours yours."

"What do you mean? Of course she's mine."

"No. I mean you're not going to be taking care of her or anything."

"Uh, yeah I am."

"Joaquin. Don't be unreasonable. We're not married—"

"That's not my fault. If it was up to me, you know we would be."

She groaned. "And that's dumb. You just don't go get married because you made a baby."

He fought to keep from yelling, but couldn't quite keep his voice calm. "How about when you love each other? Do you get married then?"

"It's a piece of paper!"

"It's so much more than that, and you know it!" He turned onto the ranch road and stepped on the gas a little more than necessary. He braked at the front of the main house. They'd all agreed to have Mother's Day lunch together—not that they usually did anything different on Sundays.

Joaquin slammed the truck into Park. "I'm part of this, Indigo. And maybe we didn't start off the way God wanted us to, but now, I guess I thought you were on the same page and we were working our way toward marriage. A family. One where you and my child were both Riveras."

Indigo stiffened. "You think I'm changing my name if we get married?"

He gave a mirthless laugh. "I thought you would, yeah. But okay, fine, you don't want to. That's fine. But the baby? She's a Rivera."

"She's a Hewitt. Or a Hewitt-Rivera."

"Seriously? You'd saddle her with some enormous hyphenated monstrosity? Even after your mom named you all Hewitts when she wasn't one herself?"

"And look where that got her!" Indigo smashed the release button her seatbelt and threw open the door. "This is why I keep changing the subject when you bring up baby names."

"Well maybe if you didn't keep dodging me, we could've had this conversation when it wouldn't have turned into a fight." Joaquin opened his own door, stepped down from the truck, and slammed it. It released a tiny bit of his frustration, but he was tempted to open the door and slam it again three or four—hundred—more times.

"Fine. You want to talk about baby names?" Indigo slammed the door on her side of the truck and marched around to stand toe to toe with him, her arms crossed and fury written on her face. "Here you go. I'll be naming the baby. You can deal with it."

She spun and started to stomp toward the house.

Joaquin grabbed her arm. "Oh no, you won't. Don't walk away. We're not done."

She yanked her arm out of his grasp and shot daggers at him with her eyes. "Yes, we are."

His gut twisted as she stormed off. Done with the conversation? Or done done? He jogged after her. "Indigo, wait."

Out of the corner of his eye, he glimpsed a car he didn't recognize—some sort of old, beat up station wagon that looked like it should be at the bottom a junk heap. The Hewitts must have invited a guest. All the more reason for him to fix this with Indigo before they got to lunch.

Indigo stopped and turned, her foot tapping.

Joaquin held up his hands. "Can we please talk this through like adults? I love you. I love my baby girl."

"*Our* baby girl."

He nodded. "Our. Please, can we just—"

"Well, well, well." The man who'd been in the junky car strode toward them. His long hair was in a thick braid that he'd slung over his shoulder. He had on corduroy pants, a denim shirt with tiny rhinestones at the shoulders, and cowboy boots. "You're a tough woman to track down, Indigo."

Joaquin scowled at the interruption. "Can we help you?"

The man's gaze barely flicked over Joaquin before visibly dismissing him. "What? No hug for your mate?"

Mate? Joaquin's mouth was dust. "Indigo?"

She'd gone pale. Joaquin reached out and gently took her arm. "Let's get you inside, honey."

"Honey, is it?" The man laughed. "I guess we'll see about that. Come on, *darling*, aren't you going to introduce me?"

Indigo shook her head and seemed to snap back. "Wingfeather. Why are you here?"

21

"What do you mean? Why wouldn't I be here?" Wingfeather shrugged and pointed to the house. "That where you're headed?"

Indigo shook off Joaquin's hand. This was a disaster. She looked at Joaquin. "Go on in. I'll be there in a minute after I see what he wants."

"I think I'd rather stay."

She closed her eyes and counted to ten then opened them again and held his gaze. "Can you please trust me to handle this?"

A mix of emotions warred briefly on Joaquin's face, and she thought she heard his teeth grinding together. Finally, he gave a curt nod, spun on his heel, and stalked toward the house.

Indigo sighed as she watched him walk away. Had she just made things even worse? They were already on shaky ground after the whole baby name conversation.

She jolted when the front door to the Hewitts' house slammed closed—the sound like a gunshot.

"Tell me again why you're here?"

Wingfeather's gaze dropped to her stomach and then back up to her face. He shook his head. "That didn't take long."

"Don't change the subject." She crossed her arms over the baby. "You disappeared. Honestly, you were gone more than you were around for the last eighteen months. But this summer you fell off the map. The cops couldn't find you. Your shaman friend wouldn't give me any clues. I figured at some point I had to take a hint. I did leave you a note. Which was more than you bothered with."

"Don't tell me you've turned into one of those people, baby. Come on, you know I need space sometimes. But I'm back now. I'd like to see my animals."

"Your animals? The ones you deserted? The ones you've done basically nothing for—up to and including paying for them. Or did you forget that I bought every single one of them?"

"We had an arrangement."

"One you walked away from and rendered void when you disappeared in July. It's been close to a year! We're done. Just go."

He shook his head and reached out to grab her arm.

Indigo stepped back, stumbling when her heel slipped on a rock.

"Everything all right out here?" Wayne's voice was clear and strong.

"This doesn't concern you, old man."

Indigo frowned at Wingfeather before turning and hurrying to stand beside Wayne. "Sorry, Grandpa. I'm not sure how he found me."

"Do you want him here?"

Indigo felt the concern and confusion in her grandfather's searching look. She shook her head. "No. I don't."

Wayne patted her arm. "Why don't you head on in? They're getting ready to serve lunch. Let them know I'll just be a minute. The sheriff's on his way."

Indigo tossed one last look over her shoulder at Wingfeather before kissing Wayne's cheek. "Thanks, Grandpa."

She slipped through the door and leaned against it as her knees weakened. That hard, mean side of Wingfeather didn't come out often. He'd only hit her three times. They never talked about it after, and invariably he'd disappear then show up later and act like nothing had happened. It had been easier to just go along.

"Are you okay?" Joaquin's hands were in his pockets, and his jaw was still clenched.

"I'm fine. Why don't you go sit down and we'll eat?"

He shook his head. "I don't think so. I learned a lot about you in a really short space of time today, and I'm not sure what to do about it."

Her belly quivered. "What do you mean?"

"Really?" His eyebrows lifted. "Okay, well let's start with how you're trying to cut me out of my baby's life, and she's not even born yet."

"That's not what I'm doing."

"Isn't it? I don't get a say in her name. You're not giving her my last name even though she's my child. Are you planning to list me on the birth certificate as her father, or were you going to leave that blank, too?"

"That's not fair."

"Believe me, I know." He scowled and crossed his arms. "Then, before we have a chance to talk that through, you're pushing me aside for the guy who abandoned you in the desert."

"I didn't push you aside, and that's just a little more dramatic than what happened."

"We'll have to agree to disagree there. I'm the one you shook off."

She opened her mouth then snapped it shut. Maybe she had.

"He's all talk, and I could handle him. I don't need some cowboy swooping in to rescue me."

"If you can't tell the difference between what I was trying to do and a swooping rescue, then I guess that's on you. I thought we were a team. I guess I was wrong."

"Joaquin—"

He shook his head. "Just don't. I love you, but this clearly isn't going to work. A team—a family—means more than you're willing to give. And I'm not willing to settle for less."

"What do you mean? What are you saying?" She crossed her arms and leaned against the door again as her knees threatened to buckle.

"I'm going to be a father to my child. Other than that? We're done." His eyes were flat. "It'd be best, I think, if you visited the animals when I wasn't there. You know the schedule, so it should be easy enough for you to do."

"Joaquin—"

He turned and strode down the hall to the kitchen. She caught a snatch of muted conversation, then more footsteps. After a minute, Maria and Cyan came out of the kitchen with bowls and platters.

Maria offered her a sad smile.

Cyan stopped, scowling. "You messed up, Indigo. Big time."

"You don't even know what happened." Indigo swallowed the hot, hard lump in her throat. She couldn't even count on her brother to take her side? Her eyes filled, and she turned away.

"I know he was good for you. I know he's the father of your child. And I know you cut his heart out and stomped on it. I expected more from you. I expected better of you."

"That's enough." Maria came back out of the dining room and took the bowl Cyan was holding. "Stop this. It's your sister's life and her relationship. And if you can't see that she's hurting, too, you're an idiot. Come in and sit down. Both of you. Betsy wants us to say grace and eat. Wayne texted that the sheriff is here, so he should be in shortly."

"I'm not hungry." Indigo swiped at her cheeks, unable to keep the tears from falling.

"The baby is." Maria's voice was gentle and her touch on Indigo's arm soothed. "You need to sit and eat a little. Have some water or some juice. And just be around people who love you."

People who loved her? Indigo let Maria lead her into the dining room. She sat next to her mom and stared down at her hands while Betsy blessed the meal. Joaquin hadn't left the ranch, but he'd walked away just the same. Everyone left.

Mom reached over and squeezed Indigo's hand. "Wingfeather was here?"

Indigo nodded.

"I guess I figured he was dead."

Indigo managed a mirthless laugh and looked over at her mom. "I did, too. Of course I can't be so lucky."

"What did he want?" Mom reached for the bowl of green beans and scooped a little portion onto Indigo's plate.

"Who even knows? He talked about the animals, but he didn't pursue it. I imagine he just figured he'd see if he could either get back with me until it was time for him to go again or cause some trouble. He's never been picky about which one." Indigo stabbed a green bean and nibbled the end. Maybe that was all she deserved—someone who would come and go as he pleased. It wasn't as if she was an amazing catch.

Sure, she'd seen some similarities between herself and the woman in Proverbs 31. At the same time, Indigo was fairly certain that woman didn't manage to get herself knocked up by a man who wasn't her husband.

Wayne came back in, dusted his hands together, and sat beside Betsy. He tossed a wink at Indigo before bowing his head.

"Do you think he'll push? Try to make a claim on the herds?" Cyan frowned across the table at her.

Indigo shook her head. "He knows I paid for them. I have bills of sale—they're all in my name. He doesn't have a leg to stand on. The house we were renting was all in his name. But I paid up through the lease end before I left, so he can't even complain about that."

"He could probably be annoyed that he doesn't have a place to live anymore." Cyan reached for another roll.

Maria swatted his hand. "You could ask. I would pass them."

He shot her a boyish grin and winked. "I could reach."

In spite of herself, Indigo smiled. The two of them really were perfect for each other. All of her siblings had found good mates. She was the only one apparently incapable of finding and maintaining worthwhile relationships. "He can be annoyed about that, but he can't blame me. He's the one who disappeared. Was I supposed to renew the lease in my name just so he had a place to come back to when he decided he was ready?"

Cyan shrugged. "I don't know. I never liked the guy—I'm just trying to think it through."

"I never really did either, but the two of you seemed happy, so I was content to let it go." Mom sighed. "I'm sorry. Maybe I should have pushed a little. But it wasn't as if I was in any position to encourage you to seek something more traditional."

"It's not your fault, Mom." It was Indigo's own fault. She wasn't looking for anyone to blame. These were her decisions coming home to roost. "Can I ask you a question?"

Mom nodded. "Of course."

"Why did you give us all Dad's last name?"

Mom blinked.

The other quiet conversation around the table stopped.

Mom cleared her throat. "You're his children. Why wouldn't I?"

"We're *your* children, too." Indigo frowned. Was the patriarchal notion of last names so firmly embedded in the world that even someone as free-spirited as her mom had just gone along with it without a second thought?

"I always used Hewitt as my last name. Never changed it legally, but it's still on my driver's license. We hit up a small town when we were newly together. They were easy enough to distract when it came to providing the documentation they needed—maybe your father slipped the clerk some cash. Regardless, at the end of the day, my official ID has Hewitt as my last name and has for years." Mom shrugged. "When you kids were born, it was never an issue. We might not have been married, but your father and I were a family."

Indigo nodded. A family was what Joaquin said he was looking for. What he said he was going to be for this baby.

She wanted freedom—from men like Wingfeather, from financial worries, from the consequences of her bad decisions.

Was it even possible to have it all?

Indigo looked down at her mostly untouched plate and scooted back from the table. "I'm sorry. I need to go lie down."

"Are you okay? Do you want me to walk back with you?" Mom dabbed her lips with a napkin and started to stand.

"No, Mom. I'm fine. You stay and enjoy your meal. Thank you for being a good mom." Indigo leaned over and pressed her lips to her mom's cheek. "Happy Mother's Day."

Mom looked like she was going to argue, but Cyan gave a quick head shake. At least he understood that Indigo just needed some time.

Maybe a nap would make everything clearer.

If nothing else, it would buy her a couple of hours where she didn't have to think about how easy she was to leave.

22

J oaquin stomped the dirt off his boots before stepping through the door of his cabin. He'd always loved the fact that work at the ranch happened—to one degree or another—every day of the week. Animals didn't stop eating or needing a clean place to live just because it was Saturday. Or because tomorrow was Father's Day. Not that it mattered.

"Hey, man."

Joaquin turned and saw Tommy lift a hand. He returned the wave. "Hey. You get that clogged drain at the camp fixed?"

"Yeah, finally." Tommy shook his head. "Some kid dropped his mother's bead necklace down the toilet and flushed. It kind of let water through, so it took some time to build up into a full clog. Bet you can guess how exciting it was to clear."

Joaquin's gorge rose. "Ugh."

"Yup. Now I want an ice-cold drink and something mindless. You busy tonight?"

"Why would I be?"

Tommy shrugged. "No reason. Except, I mean, it's been more than a month, man. Aren't you going to at least try and make things up with Indigo?"

He hadn't thought his heart could break any more than it already had, but another little piece seemed to crack off and dissolve into rubble. He shook his head. "There's no point. The next time I talk to her, I'm going to have the paperwork from my lawyer to hand her. And that's all I'm going to be talking about."

"You're really going through with that?"

Joaquin jerked his head toward the kitchen. "Come in and let's get that drink. I could use something myself."

Tommy cleaned his boots and stepped out of them before coming in. He closed the door and padded to the kitchen.

"Grab a seat. I have Coke."

"That'll work. So, the lawyer."

Joaquin took two bottles of Coke out of the fridge and popped off the tops before handing one to Tommy. He sighed and sat, dragging one of the empty chairs around to prop his feet on. "Yeah, I'm doing that. I want to see my child. And I want Indigo to know going into this that I'm going to fight her. I'll spend every dime I make—and I'll find ways to make more if that's what it takes—to ensure that I get at least fifty percent custody. She's living here, so there's no reason for her to object. We're two cabins away. It's not going to disrupt school or anything."

"I just think maybe you'd do better trying to sweet talk her into forgiving you."

"I didn't do anything wrong." Joaquin set his Coke down with more force than was necessary. A tiny bit of soda sloshed out of the top onto his hand. He wiped it on his jeans. "What last name does your daughter have?"

"Mine. But we were married."

Joaquin shook his head. "Shouldn't matter. And I offered, but she said no. Which makes more sense now that I realize she was planning on cutting me out of things completely."

"You don't know that." Tommy tipped his bottle up and took

several long swallows. "There's a lot more to having kids than naming them."

"True. But who gets to decide what I can help with and what I can't? I don't feel like that should be her choice. And that's the point. I'm going to be involved. All the way involved. If I have to serve her with legal papers to do that, then that's what I'm going to do." Joaquin drained his Coke and stood. He tossed the bottle into the recycling and grabbed a bag of chips from the top of his fridge. "Look, man. I know you have your reasons for the way you're doing things with your ex. You also know I don't agree with them. But just because you've decided that's how you're going to handle things doesn't make it right for everyone else."

Tommy looked away. "You think I like this? You think I chose it this way?"

"I don't know. It doesn't seem like you're willing to fight. She threatens and you back off."

"It's not that simple. Her family . . . there's just no way."

Joaquin shrugged. "At least with Indigo I don't have that to worry about. So I'm fighting. And I'm starting early."

"I guess maybe I'm a little jealous." Tommy reached for the chips and pulled out a handful. "This all you have to eat?"

Joaquin snorted. "I can make sandwiches. I have a ton of meat and cheese. Pickles."

"Yeah, why not. Mustard?"

"Yuck. No. Why would I have that?"

"Because you're not a toddler? It's fine. Tell me you have mayo."

"And ranch."

"On a sandwich?" Tommy shook his head. "It's a miracle you've lived to adulthood the way you eat."

"Hey now, my mom was the one who taught me to put ranch on my bread, so watch it. I might not see her much, but she's still my mom."

Tommy laughed. "What the heck, I'll try it."

Joaquin grinned and the weight he'd been carrying around on his shoulders lightened. "We need to do this more often."

"So we always say." Tommy grabbed another handful of chips. "And then the reality of ranch life gets in the way. What should we play?"

"We could watch a movie, if you didn't want a video game."

"Please."

Joaquin grabbed two plates and the bread and started assembling thick, manly sandwiches. "Call of Duty?"

"Yeah, why not? We haven't done that in a while."

"Perfect." The evening was shaping was up to be the best in a long time. A little over a month, in fact. Maybe tonight he could remember for more than twenty minutes that he'd be okay without Indigo in his life.

This was better. For both of them.

It had to be.

"I WISH you'd come in to lunch with everyone, Joaquin." Wayne had his hands in his pockets as he leaned against the porch rail of Joaquin's cabin. "Don't you think it's been long enough?"

"No, sir. I don't. I'm sorry. I appreciate the offer." Joaquin turned the handle and started in. At least Indigo had been smart enough to start going to church with her mom and the Hewitts. He'd been dreading having to change churches if she'd insisted on wanting to continue attending there. "It's better this way, in the long run."

"I don't think you're right." Wayne frowned. "I can't help but think you're making a huge mistake."

Joaquin shrugged. There was a small part of him that agreed. He still ached for Indigo. He'd found a number of places around the ranch where he could hide and watch her without risking detection. He just hadn't decided if his insistence on visiting those spots was a sign of masochism or some strange brand of exposure therapy.

"Do you love her?"

"It doesn't matter."

"Seems to me it's one of the few things that matters most."

Joaquin frowned. "Not really. She doesn't love me back."

"I think you're wrong."

He huffed out a breath. "Wayne, I appreciate you trying. I do. And I love working here and being a part of the ranch, but if fixing things with Indigo has somehow become a requirement of my employment, I'd prefer you just said so straight out."

Wayne's eyebrows winged up. "It hasn't. I'm sorry. I just hate seeing two people I love miserable, but I'll just butt back out."

Joaquin closed his eyes and counted to ten. "I told her I loved her. More than once. A lot of times. She never once said the words back. I'd get a thank you. Maybe a smile. Never words of any sort that suggested she was feeling the same thing. Okay?"

"Usually it's the man who struggles with the words."

Joaquin snorted out a laugh. "Yeah. Anyway, between that and the fact that she's trying to cut me out of our baby's life, I think it's clear there's no future where we're together. Even if I wish I could say otherwise. Throw in the fact that she wasn't in any hurry to explain to her old flame that she was with someone new if you need a cherry on the top of it all."

"Wingfeather's gone. He took off when the sheriff showed up. Seems there's a warrant for his arrest." Wayne's smile was thin and sharp. "And Indigo made it clear he wasn't welcome. I guess you'd gone inside by then."

"She made it clear I wasn't necessary." Joaquin shook his head. "Just let it be, Wayne, please? I'm expecting paperwork from my attorney tomorrow via FedEx. I'll have to deal with her for that, but otherwise it's best all around if we all just let it be."

"Paperwork?"

"I can talk to you about it tomorrow. After. Or she can. But I'd just as soon she not have any advance warning."

Wayne looked at Joaquin, offense bristling in every feature.

"Sorry. But she's your granddaughter. Blood's thicker." It was something that had been proven over and over as far as Joaquin was concerned. It was why he was going to fight for his daughter. She was his blood. If Indigo wanted to be stubborn about a relationship with him, that was fine. But being part of his daughter's life wasn't negotiable.

"I'm sorry you feel that way. I'm sorry you think I feel that way." Wayne knocked on the railing before turning toward the main house. He looked over his shoulder. "You're still welcome to Sunday lunch—especially now that Maria has bullied her way back into the kitchen. Have you even met the baby yet? We also miss you at weekday lunches. You're a part of the family here. We love you."

Joaquin offered a tight smile as his stomach twisted. He wanted to believe that. He missed seeing everyone. He missed Maria's cooking. He'd like to meet Cyan and Maria's baby, for that matter. But it was all Hewitts there these days, with the exception of Tommy, and he had to figure they were all on Indigo's side.

Even if they didn't know the details.

He sighed and headed into his cabin, kicking the door shut behind him. He set his Bible on the kitchen table and stumbled through a disjointed prayer. All his prayers were that way these days. He didn't have the words. He had thoughts. And a word here or there. But they weren't coherent, at least not to him.

He was banking on Paul being right about the Holy Spirit interceding for him, because he didn't know what to say.

The paperwork that was coming wasn't going to go over well. He knew that as sure as he knew the sun would rise in the East. There just didn't seem to be any other option.

He wasn't going to be shut out. It was too important.

He glanced at the TV and the Xbox and frowned. Maybe he could lose himself in a quest of some sort for a little while.

At least when he was gaming, he was in control of whether he won or lost. With everything else in his life, it sure seemed like he was at the mercy of someone else, pushed around by random whims.

Somewhere in the back of his mind, he knew better. He knew God was in control.

He also didn't understand why it was taking so long for Him to fix this mess.

"Jesus, if there's something I'm supposed to be doing that I'm not, would You please make it clear? Cause I'm lost. And it sure feels like I'm alone."

23

Indigo slipped one of the booties she'd knitted onto the baby, then the other. She smiled up at Maria. "See? So cute."

"I still think she's going to kick them off before—" The baby wiggled her feet and one bootie flopped off and fell on the floor of the fiber cabin. Maria laughed.

"Okay, well, we'll just try again." Indigo leaned over to pick up the bootie. Her hand slid around to the small of her back as she straightened. She put the shoe back on and tightened it. Maybe that would keep it on a little longer. "And if nothing else, the blanket and hat still work."

"They do. And they're beautiful. You're making some for your own little one, aren't you?"

"I still have time." She'd made a couple of blankets. The hat and booties were a test pattern that she obviously needed to tweak still. "Eight weeks to go."

"They'll be over before you know it. Have you thought about names yet?" Maria adjusted her daughter, chuckling as the shoe fell off again. "Let's go sit. Then if it drops, it'll be into my lap."

"Can I hold her?" Elise set the roving she'd just removed

from the drum carder aside and folded her hands in front of herself. "It's okay if you want to say no."

"Of course you can hold her, Grandma." Maria transferred the baby to Elise's eager arms before settling on the couch with a sigh. She ran a hand over the throw that was draped over the back. "This is lovely. You made this?"

Indigo nodded and sat on the chair she used for spinning. "I need to get it listed online, but I like it so much I've been dragging my feet."

"I can see why." Maria touched it again. "I'd love to have the talent you have."

Indigo snorted. "You're talented in your own right."

"Please. I can't do anything like this."

"Sure, but I can't cook. Most of the time I don't burn grilled cheese. I can do simple things, as long as I pay attention. But you? You're an artist." Indigo was going to have to do better when it was time to feed a child. At least, from what the books said, she had a year or so before it was big issue. Joaquin was a decent cook—still nothing like Maria—and that wasn't a productive train of thought. He'd taken avoiding someone to new heights.

Maria just shook her head. "Anyone can learn to do that."

"I could say the same about knitting."

Elise nodded. "She's teaching me. And Jade. She could probably teach you, if you wanted."

"I don't have time for another hobby, but I'll keep it in mind. For now, I'm glad to be able to admire what you do." Maria looked around the cabin. "You have a fun space here."

"I wish we got more walk-in business." Indigo frowned. Should she start looking for a space in town? Maybe being online was enough. They did a good business that way. "But it's fine."

The bell at the top of the door jingled.

Indigo looked over and everything seemed to freeze. Her heart stopped, then took off at a hundred miles an hour as Joaquin stepped in. He held a thick manila envelope.

"Ladies." He nodded before zeroing in on Indigo. "Can I speak to you a moment?"

"Sure." She didn't move.

"Privately?"

Her mouth was dry. "Um. Sure. I guess let's just step outside?"

He nodded once and went back out the door.

Mom reached over and squeezed Indigo's hand.

Maria shot her a bolstering smile. "This is good. Right? It has to be good."

The sinking in Indigo's stomach didn't really suggest that this was going to go well. She forced herself to stand and walk to the door. In her head she heard the *Star Wars* "Imperial March" playing ominously.

She swallowed and, after a quick prayer for help, stepped outside.

"This is for you." Joaquin thrust the envelope at her and started to turn.

Indigo grabbed it so it didn't fall, but drew her eyebrows together. "Wait."

He turned and cocked his head to the side.

"Joaquin. I . . . this is all . . ." She bit her lip. Now that he was finally here in front of her, she didn't know how to say what needed to be said.

He frowned. "Read that. You know where to find me."

She watched as he stalked off. When he was out of sight, she sank to the step, still clutching the envelope to her chest. That had not gone well. In fact, she'd be hard pressed to figure out a way for it to have gone worse.

She pounded a fist into her forehead. "Stupid."

With a sigh, Indigo bent the prongs that held the envelope's flap closed and slid out a thick packet of paper. She frowned. The law offices of . . . what *was* this? She flipped the top page up and started shaking her head as she scanned the pages.

No.

No no no no no.

She looked up and hunted for any sight of Joaquin. Now, at least she understood why he'd taken off. The chicken. How *dare* he?

She levered herself up—nothing quite so ungainly as trying to stand when pregnant. And why wasn't that in any of the books? Probably because they assumed you'd been around someone who was expecting a child before you found yourself in the same situation.

She went back into the cabin and slammed the door behind her. The jingling bells were a crazy cacophony instead of their usual cheerful welcome. She was tempted to open the door and slam it again, just to hear the noise one more time.

"That was fast." Elise jiggled the baby, who had started to cry when the door slammed.

Indigo winced. "Sorry. I—I didn't think. She's okay?"

Maria shrugged. "Sure. She's been startled before. But I agree with your mom—I kind of figured you'd be out there longer."

Indigo had thought that, too. Of course, she'd been thinking this was Joaquin coming to try and reconcile with her—did he not feel the same way she did? She snorted. So much for all his protestations of love. "All he was doing was dropping off this."

Indigo tossed the paper onto the sofa and strode across the room, hands bunched into fists at her sides.

"What is it?" Mom's voice was tentative and full of concern.

Indigo spun around. "I didn't read it yet. Not all the way. But it's from a lawyer."

"A lawyer?" Maria frowned. "Why would he talk to a lawyer?"

"Go ahead." Indigo gestured to the papers. "Read it and see if you can make heads or tails of it."

Indigo kicked the wall. She'd spent the last six weeks regretting basically every word she'd said on Mother's Day. She'd second-guessed. Thought up amazing apologies but then chickened out when she was two steps away from his door. And Joaquin? Apparently, he'd been busy talking to his lawyer.

"This is actually kind of romantic."

Indigo stared at Maria. "Papers from a lawyer are romantic?"

"Kinda?" Maria hunched her shoulders. "Hear me out here."

Indigo glanced over at her mom.

Mom lifted her eyebrows and continued rubbing the baby's back.

"All right. Let me have it."

"First, to be clear, I haven't read every word in here, and I'm not a lawyer."

"Yeah, yeah, enough disclaimers. Get on with it." Indigo smiled to soften her words. It wasn't as if she wasn't going to read every word on those papers at least once. Gosh, did she need her own lawyer now, too? Ugh. Like she had money to throw around on legal fees.

Maria offered a sympathetic smile. "Basically, it looks like he's suing for fifty-fifty custody of the baby when she's born."

"He's *suing* me?" Indigo threw her arms in the air and yanked at her hair. "And you think this is romantic?"

"Not *suing* suing. It's a legal term." Maria blew out a breath. "Focus on the custody thing. That's sweet, right? Romantic? Even though you kicked him out of your life, he still wants to do the right thing for the baby. That's the sign of a good man, right there."

Indigo gaped. She turned to look at her mom. "Mom?"

"Oh. I don't want to get in the middle of this." Mom stood, still patting the baby. "I think Cara and I are going to just go for a little walk."

"Chicken."

Her mom simply smiled and walked in the swaying, bouncing way of women holding infants. She was singing quietly and, after a moment, Indigo pinned it as one of the worship choruses she'd heard at her grandparents' church that weekend.

Indigo put her hands on her hips and looked at Maria. "You're really not on my side here?"

"I'm on the baby's side."

"That's a cop-out."

Maria shook her head.

"No way. You *know* that's a cop-out. You have to."

"I don't. I'm sorry it hurts you, but I know firsthand how hard it is to be a single mom. I understand, maybe better than you do right now, what it is to know that the only person caring for this helpless, screaming child is me. The idea that you could have help? That you'd get a break every other week? Girl. You can't put a price on that." Maria stood with a sigh. "You need to read through this. You need to pray about it. And about your relationship with Joaquin. Because the only thing better than what it looks like he's proposing in here would be for the two of you to get married and make a family."

Ugh. Indigo scowled at her sister-in-law's back as she headed down the hall to find Mom and the baby. Was this really something she was supposed to be praying about? Wasn't prayer for the big things that she couldn't handle on her own? Or, well, no. Now that she stopped to think, that wasn't what she'd seen her grandparents do. Or Joaquin. Or her siblings. They were always praying for dinky things—even blessing a meal before eating it was kind of a stupid thing to bother God about.

So. Maybe it wasn't bothering Him?

With a weary sigh, Indigo moved to the couch and picked up the packet of papers. She sat down and stared unseeingly at the cover letter.

She was messing this up, wasn't she?

She didn't know how to pray. Or what to pray about—were there rules somewhere? A list? Or was she just supposed to pray about everything? Did she need to start asking for Jesus to tell her what to wear in the morning? Surely that was taking it too far. Wasn't it?

With a frustrated growl, she stood back up, clutching the papers to her chest. "Could one of you stick around here? I need to go up to the main house for a few minutes."

"I'll be here, honey." Mom came to the junction of the hallway and the main room and offered a smile. "Take as long as you need."

"Thanks, Mom." Indigo started toward the door. She stopped and turned back. "You think it's romantic, don't you?"

Mom closed her eyes. "Let's just say I think it tells you a lot about the kind of man Joaquin is if you're willing to listen."

Indigo nodded. It did. It reinforced everything she already knew about him.

He was a good man. He'd be a great father.

She was an idiot.

24

"I can't sign this." Indigo slapped the manila envelope with his lawyer's address on the mailing label onto the hood of his truck.

In the week and a half since he'd given her the papers, Joaquin had been dreading this moment. He stepped back from the cab and shut the door, hooking his thumbs in his front pockets in an effort not to look defensive. "Why not?"

She looked away. "You're not going to make this easy, are you?"

Make it easy? He bristled. He was supposed to make it easy on her, somehow, by what? Ignoring his obligations? Turning his back on the baby they'd made together? The baby he already loved? He swallowed down the angry words that crowded onto his tongue. "Why don't you explain what you don't like, and we can talk about some compromises."

Indigo shook her head.

"Look, Indigo, you've gotta give me something to work with." He hated that he could hear the hurt in his voice. She didn't need to know that he was dying inside. She didn't need to know how much he still loved her, even though he desperately wanted not to. They needed to arrive at an acceptable business arrangement. That was it. Friendly co-parents. He cleared his throat. "Why don't you come in, and we can talk it through?"

He climbed the steps to his cabin and went inside without looking to see if she'd follow him. He wanted to throw himself at her feet and beg her to take him back, but he wasn't going to. If she didn't love him, he would deal with that. Right now, the baby was what mattered.

Joaquin opened the fridge and pulled out a Coke bottle. He heard her quiet, hesitant steps and looked over at her. "I have lemonade. Maria brought a pitcher down the other day. I guess she got mixed up and used real sugar, so Calvin shouldn't have it."

Indigo sat down at the kitchen table with a short nod. "Sure. That sounds good."

Joaquin put the Coke back and reached for the plastic pitcher instead. He got glasses down from the cabinet and carried them over to the table. "I have some chips?"

"No. That's fine. I don't need—" She sighed and pointed to the chair. "Just sit down, okay?"

He did as instructed, and poured the lemonade into the glasses. It was all so stilted and awkward. Maybe he should have tried to talk to her—again—before going to the attorney, but it felt like they would've ended up here anyway.

Indigo pushed the envelope across the table.

He rested his fingers on it. "We need something in place, Indigo. It doesn't have to be exactly this, but there has to be something. I'm not going to end up like Tommy, begging for scraps, when it comes to my kid."

"I don't want that either." She blew out a breath. "I'm sorry. I'm sorry for how I handled things on Mother's Day. For being stubborn about the name and not thinking about how you might feel when I pushed you to go inside so I could handle

Wingfeather. I was scared. Which isn't an excuse. Just an explanation."

He was frozen in place. What was she saying? His heart picked up its pace. Could she possibly . . . no. That was ridiculous. Finally, he nodded once. "Okay."

"Say you'll forgive me. Please?"

"I do. I forgive you. It doesn't change the fact that I want to be a part of the baby's life." And hers. But he couldn't say that. He didn't dare even hope that she might want that.

"I want that, too." She swallowed and looked away. When she looked over, her eyes were shiny. "I was hoping, maybe, we could go back to where we were. Or start over—if that's what you need, we can just start over. I'm hoping, maybe, you'd be willing to skip that, though. I'm hoping that maybe it's not too late for me to tell you I love you."

"You love me?"

She nodded. "I do. I have for months. Since the baby moved, at least. You're an incredible, amazing man, and I haven't appreciated that. I'm so used to being on my own—even when I was with Wingfeather, I was on my own. And so I didn't think you were going to stay. No one ever has. Not really. But you're the kind of man who sticks. And I'm hoping—praying—it's not too late for you to want to stick with me."

He stared at her, his heart hammering in his chest.

"Or not." She started to stand, and a tear slipped down her cheek. "I get that. I do. It's a lot to ask."

Joaquin jumped to his feet, and his chair clattered to the floor. He took two long strides around the table and pulled her into his arms. "It's not too much to ask. It's only everything I've ever wanted. I love you."

"I love you." She tipped her head and held his gaze. "I'm so sorry."

"I'm sorry, too. I imagine there are things we both could have done better." He rested his cheek on the top of her head. It was heaven having her in his arms. And yet. The baby was kicking, he smiled slightly as he felt his little girl's feet. "Does that hurt?"

"What? Oh, the baby?" Indigo chuckled. "Not really. Not now, at least. Sometimes she gets something more sensitive, and it gives me a moment."

Joaquin stroked the side of her belly.

"That got her to stop." Indigo shook her head. "Dad's got the touch, I guess."

"About that."

"About what?"

"The baby. I still—I love you, Indigo, but what happens if this doesn't work out?" He gave her a quick squeeze before releasing her and pacing away. He dragged a hand through his hair. "We still need to have paperwork in place. To protect all three of us."

"You're not understanding me." She blew out a breath and muttered, "Of course you're not understanding me. That would've been too easy."

He frowned. "I don't—"

"I'm asking you to marry me. I guess I was hoping I might not have to say the words. That you might get the hint and ask me. Again." She offered a sheepish shrug. "I love you. I want a life with you, where you're the father to our child in every way. And yeah, I guess there's a possibility that things might not work out, but let's give it a chance."

He grinned and scooped her up—even eight months pregnant she wasn't that heavy—and did one gentle spin. "You really want that?"

"I do." She grinned. "See? I know my line."

He laughed and everything in him lightened before he crushed his mouth to hers. And then there was no room in his mind for anything but her.

"MARRIED, HUH? CONGRATS, MAN." Morgan hefted a bale of hay onto his shoulder and carried it out to his pickup. He set it in the bed and dusted off his hands. "When are you going to propose?"

Joaquin frowned. "I don't—she proposed. Yesterday."

"Uh-huh. And does she have a ring?" Morgan reached for another hay bale.

"We can deal with that later. I'm guessing her hands are too swollen right now anyway. She was saying it was getting tricky for her to knit. The doctor's keeping an eye on it. I guess it can indicate a problem, but so far it's just normal pregnancy swelling."

Morgan put the hay in the truck and crossed his arms. "You know I proposed to Skye a year ago today."

Joaquin nodded. "Yeah, I was there, man. Fireworks bursting overhead. Classy."

Morgan chuckled. "And Skye was never someone who made a big deal about needing all the trappings."

"What are you getting at?"

"I'm just saying, every woman wants a proposal. She may never say she wants it. She might not even *know* she wants it. But trust me on this, she does. Down to the sparkling gemstone of some sort on her finger." Morgan shook his head. "Trust me on this."

Joaquin studied Morgan. The guy was smug—as all newly married guys tended to be, as far as Joaquin was concerned. Except, maybe he had the inside track on it. Morgan was married, Joaquin was not. "You really think so? Even in today's world? I mean, she asked me. What happens if I ask her and offer her a ring and she gets bent out of shape because of the patriarchy or something?"

Morgan snorted out a laugh. He held up a hand. "I'm not

saying there's no chance. I guess it's possible. Seems unlikely to me, though. Maybe you should ask Skye. Get a sister's opinion on the matter."

Joaquin groaned. "I guess. I have to head over to the camp anyway—I lost the toss with Tommy for the cabin shower that quit working."

"Lucky you." Morgan shook his head. "Don't be surprised if she mentions the fencing by the archery range."

"What's wrong with the fencing?"

"There's a big section that fell down."

"How?" Joaquin and Tommy had spent the best part of a Saturday installing that fencing two, maybe three weeks ago. "It was solid."

"Don't shoot the messenger, man. I just know the group that's out there this week brought back pictures, and it's definitely broken."

"I'll take a look." Joaquin shook his head. Knowing that it was broken now would, at least, save him some time. He'd load up what he might need to fix it—and the shower—before he headed that way. And he'd find Skye and see if she had insight into her sister's brain when it came to engagements.

Why did everything have to be so complicated?

When the truck was loaded, he headed over to the camp. Should he go fix things first, or look for Skye? Which one was more important?

He stopped in front of the main lodge and threw the truck into park. He'd go find Skye first—if nothing else to let her know he was going to fix the shower and the fence.

Joaquin strode up the steps and into the lodge. He glanced around the large common room. Empty. Not that he expected Skye to be hanging around waiting for him. She kept an office in the back—maybe she was there.

He poked his head in the kitchen on his way past. Someone

had burnt lunch. He wrinkled his nose at the smell and walked on to the far corner where Skye had turned what was a secondary pantry into an office. He rapped on the doorframe.

"Hey, Joaquin. Morgan told you about the fence?"

"Yeah. And Tommy mentioned the shower." He glanced over his shoulder down the empty hall. "I, uh, wondered though if you had a second."

"Sure. The group is out doing stations right now—there's a hike up to the peak, a creek walk, some archery, and I think maybe a group headed down to do horse riding in the ring. Point being, no one will be back till dinner."

"Jade?"

"Went on the hike, if you can believe it." Skye shrugged. "She's enjoying being here and they said it'd be nice to have another adult around."

Good. That was good. Jade would probably have some ideas, too, but Joaquin wasn't sure he wanted her input. He didn't really want to ask Skye. But now that Morgan had planted the idea in his head, he wasn't going to be able to let go. "Okay. Here's the thing. You know Indigo and I fixed things up?"

Skye grinned. "I'm so glad, too. You're right for each other."

He wanted that to be true. "Anyway—has she mentioned that she asked me to marry her?"

"What? No! That's so great! You're engaged? Why wouldn't she say something?" Skye sprang out of her chair and threw her arms around Joaquin. "Do you have a date yet? Oh! I need to seriously talk to my sister."

Joaquin eased back. "Slow down a second. I was talking to Morgan, and he suggested that maybe it didn't count. That Indigo was basically just letting me know that it was okay for me to propose, because she'd say yes. So now I'm not sure what to do."

Skye frowned. "You said she asked you?"

He nodded. "That's how I remember it."

"What did she say? As close to word for word as you can remember."

He huffed out a breath. It was yesterday. And okay, sure, that wasn't that long ago. But still. "I think it was along the lines of 'I'm asking you to marry me.' That's pretty clear, right? She asked. So I don't have to."

"Well." Skye drew the word out into two syllables.

Joaquin groaned.

"It's just that I think every little girl grows up thinking about what their proposal is going to be like. Or at least that they're going to get one."

"She did, though. I asked her to marry me in December. She said no."

"Joaquin."

"Fine." He grimaced. "So I need to ask her? She's not going to be mad because I'm taking away her agency or something like that?"

Skye laughed. "You really do know my sister. In this case, though? No. I don't think that's going to be a problem."

"Fantastic." Hopefully Skye heard the sarcasm, because nothing else he could think to say was going to work any better. "Thanks for your help."

"Sorry. I guess you were hoping for a different answer."

He shrugged. "I wanted the right answer. We're finally back on track. I don't want to mess it up because I didn't understand her proposal didn't count."

"It counted."

"Uh-huh. That's why I have to do it again." Joaquin shook his head and started down the hall. "I'll get the shower and the fence fixed up."

"Thanks. And hey, Joaquin?" He turned. Skye had her head poking around the doorframe. "She likes rubies."

Rubies. He touched his forehead with two fingers in a mock salute. Maybe a ruby would be cheaper than a diamond. He didn't care about the cost so much—he wanted Indigo to be happy.

But he also wanted to be done with all the second guessing. He loved her. She loved him. Was it ever going to be as easy as it seemed like it ought to be?

25

I ndigo stared, slack jawed, at her sister Skye. "You told him what?"

"Why are you mad? I'm helping." Skye reached out and rubbed a skein of yarn hanging on the wall. "This is soft."

"It's alpaca. Don't change the subject. You made Joaquin think that he has to ask me to marry him. For the third time. How is that helping?"

"Well, I told him I figured it was a safe bet you'd say yes now." Skye took the yarn down off the wall and rubbed it to her cheek. "Morgan would look good in this color. Maybe if I start now, I can figure out crochet before Christmas, and I could make him a scarf and hat."

"It's not going to take you five months to figure out how to crochet a scarf and hat." Indigo huffed and pointed to the pattern booklets on a spinning rack in the corner. "I can help you. And it'll actually be helpful as opposed to what you did."

"I also mentioned you prefer rubies to diamonds. You're welcome."

Indigo buried her face in her hands. Could this get any worse? "I want to believe you meant well."

"I did." Skye made a sound suspiciously like "hrumph" and gave the rack a hard spin. Patterns cascaded to the floor. She sighed, stopped the rack, and squatted. "Sorry. About all of it. Morgan's the one who put the idea in his head in the first place."

Great. Now her brother-in-law thought she was a harridan, too. Not that Joaquin thought that anymore. Hopefully. She groaned. "I wish you'd left it alone."

"You'll say yes, won't you?"

"Of course, I will." Indigo marched to the rack, took the stack of patterns from her sister, and flipped through them. She pulled out an easy hat and scarf crochet combo and handed it to Skye before returning the others to their place on the rack. "But he doesn't have to ask again. As far as I'm concerned, we're engaged. I'll talk to him about it tonight at the fireworks."

Skye frowned. "Just let him ask you. You ought to have some romance in your life."

"I have plenty. Thanks." Indigo huffed out a breath. Her sister meant well. How many times was she going to have to repeat that to herself? "Let it go, okay? My life is obviously not the same as yours. And that's all right."

"I just don't see why—"

"You don't need to. Stop, okay? Let me see that pattern, and I'll find you a hook." Indigo held out her hand.

"Fine. I'm sorry, I guess." Skye gave one shoulder a bad-tempered jerk. "I just want my niece to have two parents."

"She does. Even if I didn't end up with Joaquin, she'd have two parents. It's not like she appeared in a cabbage patch."

"You know what I mean."

Indigo grinned. "I do. And I'm reminding myself, again, that you mean well. But I'm also starting to wonder if maybe you'd like me to start interfering in your life to remind you how great it is. Should I ask when you and Morgan are going to provide Mom with some grandchildren?"

Skye shook her head and held up her hands, palms out. "No. Fine. I get it. I'm sorry, okay?"

Indigo nodded. "Better. Look, we just need to figure this out for ourselves."

"I guess. But asking him to marry you so he wouldn't take you to court isn't exactly the kind of story you tell your kids."

Was that how Skye thought it went down? Did they all think that? Okay, sure, that was part of it, but it wasn't like it was the reason. "I love him. He loves me. Just mind your own."

"Yeah, yeah." Skye took the hook Indigo handed her. "Do you have a name yet?"

"My name's Indigo. I'm your sister."

Skye rolled her eyes and pointed to Indigo's enormous belly. "For my niece. Which you knew."

"Not yet." It hadn't come up yesterday when she and Joaquin had worked things out. She wasn't in a rush to open that conversation, either. What if he wanted to name the baby a grandma name? There wasn't anything wrong with old-fashioned names —some of them were cute. Some were making a comeback. But it was all compromise and communication, and Indigo wasn't great at either of those things.

"Don't do the color thing. Please?" Skye dug money out of her pocket and held it out.

"What are you doing? Put that away." Indigo frowned at her sister. "And no, I don't plan on doing the color thing. No one who grew up like we did would go on and perpetuate that insanity."

Skye laughed and set the money on the table. "I'm paying for this. You run a business. Take the money."

"You're my sister."

"So? Take the money. You can't give everything away. I know for a fact you didn't charge Mom or Jade, and that's just not right."

"I'm doing okay."

"Now you're doing a little better." Skye checked her phone. "I have to run to the lodge—there should be people getting back before too long, and I like to be around in case they need me."

"You'll still be up on the ridge for the fireworks, though, right?"

"Of course. That's where Morgan proposed last year." Skye waggled her eyebrows.

"Go away, Skye." Indigo laughed and shooed her sister out the door. She scooped the money up and carried it over to the cashbox. Mom and Jade were up at the main house helping Maria and Betsy get ready for tonight. No one was going to come all the way out to the ranch to buy yarn on the Fourth of July. She wasn't even sure why she'd bothered opening. Except that it was a Saturday, and she'd had some spinning she wanted to get done anyway.

She might as well close up. She rubbed little circles on her belly to try and calm the baby. She was active today. Maybe she was picking up on her mom's happiness. Indigo chuckled quietly to herself as she walked through the cabin turning off lights and making sure she hadn't left anything in a state it shouldn't stay in through the rest of the weekend.

Satisfied that it was all well, Indigo collected the knitting she was working on and stuffed it into her bag before walking out and locking the door behind her.

They'd be eating on the ridge before the fireworks—so dinner was a little later than usual today. Which meant she needed a snack. She was already starving. Indigo looked down the path that would take her to her grandparents' house. There was sure to be food there—good food—but it was a long walk and the food would come with an expectation of conversation.

She just wasn't in the mood.

She turned and headed toward the cabin she and Mom shared and let her thoughts drift.

When would Joaquin want to get married? Before the baby? She blew out a breath. There were pros and cons to that, certainly. She was roughly the size of a small whale these days—so a fancy wedding dress was out of the picture. Not that that was really her style. Or anything she cared about, if she was honest. Would Mom want it? Or Grandma? They'd both seemed to roll with the various wedding choices people had made so far. So maybe she and Joaquin could just slip into town some afternoon and go to the courthouse.

That would be her preference.

Maybe he wanted that big church to-do? She wrinkled her nose.

"What's that look? You feel okay?" Joaquin appeared at her side and slipped an arm around her waist. "Let me help you."

"I'm fine. I was thinking." She chuckled and leaned against his side, her arm sliding around him. "Do you want a big wedding?"

He stopped and turned so he could hold her gaze. "Why are you asking?"

"Well, we're engaged." She nodded slowly to emphasize her words. "Right?"

He laughed and forked a hand through his hair. "Your family is confusing."

"Tell me about it. Look, I heard about Morgan and Skye ganging up on you. I don't need another proposal. Or a ring—although, to be fair, I do prefer rubies. And, since I'm laying it all out, I don't want a big wedding. I was just thinking how nice it would be if you and I could head into town, stop at the courthouse, get married, and then go get dinner."

"Really?"

"Really. And maybe that would disappoint people. I don't

know. I'm also not sure how much it should matter. Unless *you* wanted the big wedding. Which is why I asked."

He brushed his lips over hers.

Indigo closed her eyes and leaned in, her hands moving up to his shoulders.

"Mm." He stepped back and started toward the cabins. "I don't need a big wedding, but I would like a church wedding."

Her heart sank and the little bubble holding her imaginary courthouse visit popped. She swallowed. "Okay. Then we'll do that. Were you thinking before the baby? After? I don't even know if it's possible to do before the baby, it's like six and a half weeks if I go full term. Which, I mean, the doctor says that's not necessarily how things work."

"Yeah. I was reading online and babies do their own thing at the end, looks like. What if we split the difference?"

She stopped and scowled. "We're not getting married while I'm in labor."

He threw his head back and laughed. "No. That's not what I meant. Sorry. What if we talked to the pastor about getting married at the church, but not a big thing? Just some afternoon."

"Can you do that?"

Joaquin shrugged. "I don't see why not. If the pastor's on board with it. It doesn't hurt to ask."

"Can we call him now?" Indigo rubbed her suddenly sweaty hands on her pants. "It'd be nice to be able to give people an answer when they start asking about dates."

"Sure." Joaquin took his phone out of his pocket and opened a browser. Indigo watched as he pulled up the church's website and tapped the phone icon. Joaquin hit the speaker button as it rang.

It didn't take long to get connected to the pastor.

"Joaquin, it's unusual to hear from you. How can I help?"

Joaquin's chuckle was full of nerves. Indigo reached for his hand. He cleared his throat. "Well. You've met Indigo Hewitt."

"Of course. Although we've missed her the last several weeks. I heard she's been attending across town with her grand-parents."

"Yes, sir. She and I had a miscommunication."

Indigo turned a snort into a cough and looked away. That was putting it mildly.

The pastor's voice held humor. "That can happen. I also heard it might have been resolved."

"The grapevine's moving fast these days. Yeah. And the thing is, we realized it's dumb to wait. We'd like to get married."

"That's wonderful. Were you calling about premarital counseling?"

"Oh. Well that's probably a good idea. But we were also wondering if it was possible to have you marry us without the crowd. Sort of like a courthouse wedding, but at church."

There was a long pause.

Indigo bit her lip and glanced over at Joaquin. Was that a no?

"I don't see why not, though I would want to meet with the two of you a few times first. I realize the baby is probably compressing your timeline a little."

"Yes, sir."

Indigo let out her breath. At least the pastor was willing to consider it.

"Tell you what. Let's get together Monday afternoon—say three?"

Joaquin lifted his eyebrows at Indigo.

She nodded.

"Okay."

"We'll look at the calendar and go over the topics that I think every couple should talk through before they get married and see if we can hit the high points before your baby makes it on ing after."

"Thank you." Joaquin pulled Indigo to his side and kissed the top of her head. "We'll see you Monday at three."

Joaquin ended the call.

Indigo grinned and leaned up to touch her lips to his. "I love you."

"I love you, too." He searched her face. "You need to rest before the big to-do tonight."

She laughed. "How'd you know? I was heading for a snack and a rest when I bumped into you. But I can't regret the diversion."

"Come on, let's get you home." He kept his arm tight around her shoulders as they walked.

Indigo relaxed against him. He might be taking her back to the cabin, but she was already home.

26

Joaquin brushed a hand over the large turquoise circle that formed the slide for his bolo. Why was he nervous? The last month of pre-marital counseling sessions had done nothing but confirm that he and Indigo were making the right decision.

He loved her.

She loved him.

They were going to make a family and do their best to be an example of God's redemption. It wasn't always going to be easy —he got that. Their relationship had had ups and downs already, so it wasn't as if this wedding was going to somehow fix everything. But it was still exactly what he wanted.

He'd never been more sure of anything in his life.

Which brought him back to the question: why was he nervous?

"You all right?" Tommy grinned and brushed at Joaquin's shoulders. "You look snazzy. Dark grey suit was a good choice."

"It's what I had." Joaquin shrugged. "Indigo was okay with it."

"You ready?"

Joaquin blew out a breath and shot up a quick prayer for peace before nodding. "Yeah. I am. I think this is right where God wants me to be."

"Then let's go get you married. The pastor sent me back here to tell you he was set."

Showtime. Joaquin took a deep breath and stepped through the door at the side of the stage. Usually the worship team used the door when they were getting set to start the service. Today, it took him out to stand beside the pastor. He smiled and turned to glance out at the sanctuary. It was empty, save for everyone who lived at Hope Ranch. His parents hadn't been able to get away.

"Ready?" The pastor's whisper drew Joaquin's attention back to him.

"I am."

The pastor grinned and signaled the pianist.

The door at the back of the sanctuary opened. Skye came down first. When she'd reached the front, the music changed. Everyone stood and turned toward the back. Indigo stepped through the doors and Joaquin's heart stopped.

She was gorgeous.

Her dress was simple with a snug top that cinched under her bust and a flowing skirt that draped over her pregnant belly. She was glowing.

Indigo held a bouquet of daisies and she strode down the aisle faster than the music.

He fought a chuckle and reached for her hand.

The pastor wasn't quite as successful at smothering his laugh as the music wound to an end. "Dearly beloved, we are gathered here today to witness the marriage of Indigo Hewitt and Joaquin Rivera."

Joaquin struggled to focus on the words that were said, but all he could see, all he could feel, all he could think about was Indigo.

Thankfully, since it was a Tuesday afternoon and only family was there, the pastor kept things brief. Before Joaquin knew it, he was facing his bride, both her hands in his. He reached into his pocket for the ruby and diamond band he'd found in the estate jewelry section of a store in Santa Fe. It was understated, but it would suit her.

"With this ring, I thee wed." Joaquin slipped the ring onto Indigo's finger.

Her eyes widened and her gaze flicked up to his, radiant.

He'd take that as a good sign.

Indigo turned to Skye and then back. She slid a ring with turquoise insets onto his finger. "With this ring, I thee wed."

Joaquin smiled as she finished her vows.

A few more words, and then, finally, the pastor said, "You may now kiss the bride."

Joaquin stepped forward and pulled Indigo into his arms as he lowered his mouth to hers. There were cheers and whistles.

Indigo started to laugh.

He eased back but didn't release his grip. "I love you."

"I love you, too."

"I'm pleased to introduce for the first time, Mr. and Mrs. Joaquin Rivera." As the pastor finished speaking, the piano began to play.

Joaquin turned back to the pastor and extended his hand. "Thank you."

"It's my pleasure. I'm praying for you two. I want you to know my door is always open."

"Thanks." Indigo leaned her head on Joaquin's shoulder.

Warmth spread through him and he looked down at her with a smile. She was his wife now. A year ago, if someone had told him he'd be married and expecting his first child any day, he would have laughed for hours. Now? He was simply in awe of the blessings God had given and the beauty He'd made out of

Joaquin's mistakes. Best of all? He was closer to God now than he'd ever been—and that gave him a bigger sense of freedom than he'd realized was possible.

"You ready?"

Indigo nodded and rubbed her belly. "I wouldn't mind a rest before dinner, actually. Is that okay?"

"Of course. I'm sure they'll understand." Joaquin took her hand and they stepped down to where the family was waiting with big smiles.

Elise—his mother-in-law now—had shiny eyes that went along with her mile-wide grin.

He chuckled. He was going to have to get used to the relationships shifts. It was a good problem to have. "Indigo wants to rest a little before dinner."

"Of course, honey." Elise smiled and kissed her daughter's cheek. She turned to look at Joaquin. "I'm so glad the two of you figured this out. And made it legal—and more importantly, God-honoring."

"Mom."

"No, honey. I should have pushed your father more—we should have done better. Now I can look back and see that. But you can't change the past. I'm glad the two of you are stepping into the future free from anything that's going to turn you away from God." Elise kissed Indigo's cheek a second time, then brushed her lips lightly across Joaquin's cheek. "Go. We'll see you at dinner."

"Make sure you actually let her rest, man." Cyan shot a finger out at Joaquin with a wicked glint in his eye.

"Cyan!" Indigo's face turned red and she shook her head at her brother. "That's . . . you're . . ."

Cyan laughed even as Maria punched him in the arm.

"What'd he mean, Mom?" Calvin tugged on Maria's hand.

Maria shot Cyan a look. "You can talk to your dad about that when we get home."

Cyan paled.

Joaquin laughed. Served him right. Not that the thought hadn't crossed his mind—but she was due in sixteen days. And she was starting to get that washed-out pallor that exhaustion tended to cause. "Let's get you home."

"Our home."

He looked at her. Love radiated out of her eyes. He pressed his lips to hers. "Our home."

In the truck, Indigo leaned her head against the headrest and closed her eyes.

"Are you sure you're okay?"

"Yeah. I think I just need to rest. My back is aching a little and my stomach feels off."

He frowned as he turned out of the church parking lot. "Are you coming down with something?"

"I really think I'm just tired." Indigo reached over and squeezed his hand. She drew in a short, sharp breath.

"What?"

"Braxton Hicks."

That was a contraction. Normal. Not labor. Still terrifying. "You're sure?"

She nodded.

He'd take her word for it. He had no idea. He'd read a couple of books about taking care of babies once they were out. He'd gone to the childbirth classes with her. He was still completely at sea. So he'd take her home, tuck her in bed, and maybe stretch out next to her. That, at least, was something he could do.

And naps were never a bad idea.

They'd talked about driving into Santa Fe for a fancy dinner, but Maria and Betsy had insisted they were excited about doing something big at the ranch. Neither he nor Indigo had pushed back too hard. Maria was a genius in the kitchen.

Joaquin turned into the ranch driveway and continued around the Hewitts' house toward his—now their—cabin. He and Indigo had moved her things in this morning. There was still unpacking to do, but that was easy enough, and they had time.

The baby wasn't due for two more weeks.

He shifted into Park and cut the engine. Indigo still had her eyes closed, but her face looked anything but relaxed.

"We're home."

She opened her eyes and smiled.

"I'll come around and help you down. Stay put, okay?"

"Okay. Thanks."

Joaquin hopped out of the truck and rounded the hood. He opened her door and held out his hand. "Here we go."

Indigo took his hand, leaning into him as she slid her legs over and felt for the step. She had one foot on the ground when she drew in a loud breath and a puddle of water appeared at her feet. She looked up at Joaquin, panic clear on her face. "Oh, no."

He blinked. What was—had she—that was—"Your water broke?"

Indigo nodded and started to laugh, the sound ending in a sort of strangled gasp as she clutched her abdomen.

"Not Braxton Hicks."

"No."

He couldn't move. His mind was completely blank. What was he supposed to do? The baby was coming. "I thought we had two weeks."

"I guess she decided not to wait. My bag, love. It's right inside the door. Can you get it?"

Bag. Right. The hospital bag. Now, with something concrete to do, he dropped her hand and raced up the steps to the cabin.

He reached inside for the bag at the same time he grabbed his cell out of his pocket. He hit the speed dial for Wayne.

"Hi, Joaquin." There was laughing and chattering in the background—probably everyone at the main house hanging around until their wedding supper.

"Slight change of plans. Indigo and I are heading to the hospital."

"Everything okay?"

"Everything's great. But I guess our daughter wanted to celebrate with us on the outside." He ended the call, tossed Indigo's bag into the back seat, and climbed in. He looked over at Indigo. "You ready?"

She shook her head. "No. But I guess we don't have a choice."

He leaned over and kissed her before starting the truck. "We're going to be okay. God's got this."

"Right." A tear slipped down her cheek.

"I love you, Indigo. We're going to be okay." As Joaquin drove back down toward town, he prayed. God had seen them through this far, he had to believe He'd get them the rest of the way there.

27

I ndigo pushed the door of Joaquin's truck open and sighed. It was good to be back home. The hospital, for all that they did their best to keep her comfortable, was not restful. She turned, but Joaquin was already opening the back door and unhooking the car seat from the base he'd installed.

"You got her?"

He looked up and grinned, love shining out of his eyes. For her? For the baby? Maybe—probably—both. Fatherhood suited him right down to the ground. "I've got her. Can you do the steps or do you need a hand?"

She hurt some still, but they assured her it would get better quickly. "I think I'll be okay."

"Don't push too hard." Joaquin hooked the baby carrier on his elbow and strode around to Indigo. He offered his other arm.

Indigo took it. If nothing else, it was an excuse to touch him. "This wasn't really the honeymoon I had in mind."

He chuckled. "It's all right. A few more weeks isn't going to make a difference. I love you."

"I love you, too." She took the first of three steps. It might not matter to him—and she actually doubted that—but it mattered to her. She hated that they'd started their marriage off this way. Nothing they'd done had gone according to plan. But he was right. They'd be okay.

The baby let out a mewling cry.

Indigo peered over. Elise's eyes were still closed, though her face was scrunched up as if she was considering letting out one of her ear-piercing wails. "I think she's getting hungry."

"Let's get you two inside and settled then." He reached for the cabin door and pushed it open before stepping aside to let Indigo in.

"Surprise!" Indigo's mom, Betsy, and Wayne grinned at them from the living area. "Welcome home."

Oh, boy. Company. It wasn't unreasonable that they wanted to be here and get to meet baby Elise. But gosh, she'd wanted even ten minutes to decompress. Maybe work up the energy for a shower. She pushed her lips into a smile, but it felt fake. "Hi."

Joaquin leaned close, his whisper tickling her ear. "They wouldn't take no for an answer. I'm sorry. I'll make sure they leave fast."

Indigo nodded. Her mom could be pushy when she wanted to. And having named the baby after her, well, it was a miracle Mom hadn't pushed her way into the hospital to say hello.

Indigo moved to the rocking chair that hadn't been in the living room the last time she'd been here. "This is new?"

"Well, new to you. We saw it at the church consignment shop and knew it had to come home with us." Wayne gestured for her to sit. "If I'm right, it was handmade by a local woodworking artist—it looks like his work at least."

Indigo ran a hand over the smooth, gleaming wood as she sat. "It's lovely. Thank you."

The baby let out a shriek.

"She's hungry. I just need to—" She stopped and heat flooded her face. She couldn't nurse in front of her mom and grandparents. It was awkward enough in front of Joaquin, and he was her husband. Only for two whole days, but still. She wasn't body conscious around him, that was what mattered.

"Why don't we give you some privacy?" Wayne stood and reached for Betsy's hand to help her stand.

"Oh, Wayne, she's just going to feed the baby." Betsy frowned.

"Bets." Wayne shot her a look, quieting her.

"All right. Elise? Maybe we could go down to your place and have a cup of tea."

"I—" Elise looked over at Indigo. Her shoulders fell, but she nodded. "Yes, all right. Jade's there. Maybe she'll join us."

"Thanks. I'm sorry." Indigo worked at the buckles of the baby carrier and gently lifted her daughter from the nest of blankets and straps. She waited until Joaquin had closed the door behind her family before undoing the snaps of her nursing shirt. Elise latched on greedily and Indigo's heart swelled. Nursing had happened naturally from the start—she'd been prepared to have to struggle. And while it wasn't what she'd consider comfortable, it was worth it. She brushed a hand over Elise's head and looked over at Joaquin.

He was watching her, smiling. "You're a picture."

She chuckled. "A nightmare, you mean."

"Not to me." He pulled a chair over and sat beside her. "Since we didn't let them come to the hospital, they were pretty insistent. I did convince them not to invite everyone and turn it into a party. With food."

"Like they did for Maria and Cyan?" Indigo fought a shudder. Maria had seemed to love it—but she'd been through this before. Maybe it was different the second time around. Or maybe it was a difference in their personalities. "Thank you for quashing that."

"It wasn't hard. Even your mom knew you'd hate that. Cyan,

too, for that matter. Skye and Royal just want any chance for a party, so I think they're still plotting, but maybe we can push for that to be a one-month-old thing."

"I'd like that." She dropped her head back against the chair and rocked gently as Elise nursed. She was so tired.

"You need a shower and a nap, don't you?" He frowned. "Why don't I run next door and—"

"No. You're right. They just need to meet her. But maybe . . ."

"Go on. Maybe?"

"Maybe I could grab that shower and lie down after she's done eating? They want to see Elise, not me."

"That's a fantastic idea. We'll do that." He stood and brushed a kiss across Elise's forehead and then Indigo's. "I'm going to go check on the bedroom. I'd cleaned up before the wedding, but . . ."

Indigo shook her head, carefully detached Elise, and shifted her to a good position for burping. When the baby had belched, Indigo switched sides and let her nurse some more.

Her eyes drifted closed as she rocked and nursed the baby. What was it that settled over her shoulders? She couldn't name the feeling—it wasn't one she was used to, but it very much seemed like something she'd been searching for most of her life.

Contentment.

Family.

Freedom.

She opened her eyes and watched her husband disappear into their bedroom.

Love.

EPILOGUE

J
ade stood at the edge of the living room and watched as Indigo handed her baby to her mom, kissed both of them, and made her way toward the back of the cabin.

Joaquin hovered near Elise, as if he was hesitant to trust her with the baby. And wasn't that shared name going to be hard for everyone? It was nice, probably, for Indigo to have made the baby her mother's namesake, but why?

Maybe Jade just didn't understand family.

Betsy and Wayne sat on the couch and waited their turn. They whispered to one another—probably something lovey dovey. Her grandparents had no sense of propriety. They still acted like teenagers in love. A lot. And they didn't seem to care if anyone was watching.

Open affection seemed to be a Hewitt tradition.

It sure wasn't what she was used to. None of this was.

Even as she thought it, Jade chastised herself. Her mom had done her best. It wasn't fair to criticize her. Not really. Maybe a little. Now that she saw people who actively lived out their faith, she couldn't bring herself to mock them as her mom had always done. Nor could she completely discount their beliefs.

She wasn't necessarily ready to jump in with both feet, but she was, at least, interested in learning more. And—wonder of wonders—her grandparents had invited her to stay. For as long as she wanted. When was the last time that had been offered to her?

Never, that was when.

Elise—Indigo's mom, not the baby—had even said Jade could move into the cabin she'd shared with Indigo until recently. Jade was still trying to wrap her mind around that. She'd said yes—staying with Elise seemed easier, somehow, than in the main house with Wayne and Betsy. But it was also awkward.

Which was better, really, the parents of the guy who impregnated your mom and left her to deal with it alone, or the wife he betrayed in the process? Jade shook her head.

"You can come in, you know." Joaquin gestured for her to join them. "Even hold the baby, if you want. After Wayne and Betsy get a turn."

"I don't want to intrude." Jade crossed her arms.

"Please." Joaquin shook his head and gestured for her to come forward again. "You're family."

Did they think that? Really? Without much choice, Jade moved into the living room and perched on the edge of the couch beside Wayne.

"She's a looker, isn't she?" Wayne angled the baby so Jade could see her face.

Jade nodded. There was nothing else to do, even though she thought all babies looked like grumpy old men mixed with monkeys until they were a few months old.

"You want a turn?" Wayne shifted.

"No. I don't really do babies."

"Oh, honey. Babies are wonderful. Just scoot back and let

Wayne put her in your arms." The look Betsy gave her was so full of warmth that Jade did as she was told.

The baby was light and warm and Jade could feel sweat trickling down her back. What if she dropped her? Or didn't support the head enough? Or—

"Relax. You're doing great." Joaquin studied her. "Never held a baby before?"

"Not enough to matter." Jade looked down at the baby's wide, brown eyes and something in her heart shifted.

She glanced up and looked around at the motley crew gathered. She thought of her other half-siblings and their spouses who lived on the ranch.

Maybe, just maybe, if she stuck around, she'd finally figure out where she belonged.

AUTHOR'S NOTE

My books never manage to stay light and fluffy. I love to read a good light and fluffy book, so that's not meant to be pejorative at all. And, in fact, I have set out a couple of times with the intention of writing less weighty books.

God always has other plans.

I'm learning to be okay with it—because I am deeply and heavily burdened by the world we live in. And my heart hurts not just for the unsaved, but for believers who are floundering in the world trying to figure out how to live for Jesus when the culture screams at us that doing that—being faithful to the Word—makes us bad people.

And my heart continues to be burdened by those who find themselves in churches where there doesn't seem to be an understanding that Salvation is just the beginning. We all mess up—even as believers. And God's grace is there for us, again and again, if we confess our sin. 1 John 1:9 doesn't just apply to the unsaved.

It's my hope and prayer that everyone who reads my books will realize the immeasurable depth of God's love for them. And that there is something that challenges you to think. And that we will all endeavor to live our lives for Christ from an attitude of prayer and Scripture reading. Because there is nothing more important—no book or theological talking head—than that.

Thanks as always to Valerie Comer for being a friend and Beta reader. To the gals in the Author Tribe who have let me join them and accepted me as one of their own: Tara Grace Ericson, Mandi Blake, Hannah Jo Abbott, Jess Mastorakos, and K Leah — y'all are awesome and I appreciate your friendship. (You should go read their books. Seriously.) Thanks also to Lynnette Bonner, Lee Tobin McClain, and Carol Moncado for the challenges to do more and grow as an authorpreneur. (Which is a stupid word but whatever.)

And to my family - my amazing husband and boys - thank you for all the space and encouragement you give my writing. You are and ever will be my priority, but I appreciate you letting me wiggle this in, too.

Last but never least, Jesus. Thank you for grace. For words. For stories. For loving me even when I have a hard time loving myself.

WANT A FREE BOOK?

If you enjoyed this book and would like to read another of my books for free, you can get a free e-book simply by signing up for my newsletter on my website.

OTHER BOOKS BY ELIZABETH MADDREY

Hope Ranch Series

Hope for Christmas

Hope for Tomorrow

Hope for Love

Hope for Freedom

Hope for Family

Hope at Last

Peacock Hill Romance Series

A Heart Restored

A Heart Reclaimed

A Heart Realigned

A Heart Redirected

A Heart Rearranged

A Heart Reconsidered

Arcadia Valley Romance – Baxter Family Bakery Series

Loaves & Wishes

Muffins & Moonbeams

Cookies & Candlelight

Donuts & Daydreams

The 'Operation Romance' Series

Operation Mistletoe

Operation Valentine

Operation Fireworks

Operation Back-to-School

Prefer to read a box set? Find the whole series here.

The 'Taste of Romance' Series

A Splash of Substance

A Pinch of Promise

A Dash of Daring

A Handful of Hope

A Tidbit of Trust

Prefer to read a box set? Get the series in two parts! Box 1 and Box 2.

The 'Grant Us Grace' Series

Wisdom to Know

Courage to Change

Serenity to Accept

Joint Venture

Pathway to Peace

Prefer to read a box set? Grab the whole series here.

The 'Remnants' Series:

Faith Departed

Hope Deferred

Love Defined

Stand alone novellas

Kinsale Kisses: An Irish Romance

Luna Rosa (part of A Tuscan Legacy)

Non-Fiction

A Walk in the Valley: Christian encouragement for your journey through infertility

For the most recent listing of all my books, please visit my website.

ABOUT THE AUTHOR

Elizabeth Maddrey is a semi-reformed computer geek and homeschooling mother of two who lives in the suburbs of Washington D.C. When she isn't writing, Elizabeth is a voracious consumer of books. She loves to write about Christians who struggle through their lives, dealing with sin and receiving God's grace on their way to their own romantic happily ever after.

facebook.com/ElizabethMaddrey

instagram.com/ElizabethMaddrey

bookbub.com/authors/elizabeth-maddrey

www.ingramcontent.com/pod-product-compliance
Lightning Source LLC
Chambersburg PA
CBHW030255200626
46816CB00002BA/646